St. John's College

Commemoration of the One Hundredth Anniversary of St. John's

College

1789-1889

St. John's College

Commemoration of the One Hundredth Anniversary of St. John's College
1789-1889

ISBN/EAN: 9783337402266

Printed in Europe, USA, Canada, Australia, Japan

Cover: Foto ©Andreas Hilbeck / pixelio.de

More available books at **www.hansebooks.com**

1789—1889.

Commemoration

OF THE

One Hundredth Anniversary

OF

St. John's College.

Published by the Alumni Association.

Baltimore:
PRINTED BY WILLIAM K. BOYLE & SON,
110 E. Baltimore Street.
1890.

Commemoration.

AT the meeting of the Alumni Association, held in McDowell Hall on the afternoon of the 28th of June, 1888, the matter of the celebration of the ONE HUNDREDTH ANNIVERSARY of the opening of St. JOHN'S COLLEGE, was considered, and without formal action being taken, it was placed in charge of the Executive Committee, consisting of the following persons:

> J. SHAAFF STOCKETT, *Ex-officio Chairman,*
> HUGH NELSON,
> HENRY D. HARLAN,
> L. DORSEY GASSAWAY,
> DANIEL R. RANDALL,
> J. HARWOOD IGLEHART.

In discharge of the duty thus assigned them, the Executive Committee prepared a memorial to the Board of Visitors and Governors of the College, asking their aid and co-operation; and a scheme of celebration was formulated, and submitted to them through Principal Fell, all which, together with a communication from himself upon the same subject, were, at a quarterly meeting of the Board, held on the 2nd of January, 1889, referred to their Executive Committee. In pursuance of this action a joint meeting of the Executive Com-

1

mittee of the Visitors and Governors, and of the Executive Committee of the Alumni Association, was held on the 14th of January. The members present on the part of the former were:

FRANK. H. STOCKETT,
NICHOLAS BREWER,
JOHN WIRT RANDALL,
WILLIAM G. RIDOUT.

The members present on the part of the latter were:

J. SHAAFF STOCKETT,
HENRY D. HARLAN,
DANIEL R. RANDALL.

The joint meeting was presided over by Mr. Frank. H. Stockett, President of the Board of Visitors and Governors. Mr. Daniel R. Randall was appointed Secretary. Principal Fell was present co-operating with the Committees. After an interchange of views as to the time most suitable for holding the Celebration, Wednesday, the 26th of June was selected; and a sub-committee, composed of Principal Fell, Nicholas Brewer, Henry D. Harlan, and J. Shaaff Stockett, was appointed, with authority to prepare a Programme of Exercises for the Celebration, to be submitted at a subsequent meeting of the joint Committees. This meeting took place on the evening of the 11th of February. The members present were Nicholas Brewer, L. Dorsey Gassaway, J. Harwood Iglehart, Daniel R. Randall, J. Wirt Randall, William G. Ridout, and J. Shaaff Stockett, together with Principal Fell. In the absence of Mr. Frank. H. Stockett the meeting was presided over by Mr. J. Shaaff Stockett, President of the Alumni Association. Principal Fell, as Chairman of the sub-committee, presented a Programme, which, after some modification, was accepted; but the same was subsequently further modified. On motion of Mr. Gassaway, the following persons, to constitute the Committee on Invitations, were appointed by the Chair:

THOMAS FELL,
L. DORSEY GASSAWAY,
HENRY D. HARLAN,
J. WIRT RANDALL,
WILLIAM G. RIDOUT.

The Executive Committee of the Alumni Association sent the following circular to every Alumnus whose address could be obtained:

ANNAPOLIS, MD., APRIL 15th, 1889.

DEAR SIR:
Encouraged by the success of our efforts last year, as evidenced by the pleasant Re-union and Banquet, we again address you in behalf of the Alumni Association of St. John's College.

This being the Centennial year of our ALMA MATER, it has been determined to hold a Re-union of the Alumni worthy of such an event in her history, and we earnestly request your active co-operation and assistance.

A week has been set apart for the Celebration, during which time many notable persons will be present, especially on Wednesday, ALUMNI DAY, and Thursday, COMMENCEMENT DAY, June 26th and 27th.

The Banquet will be held in McDowell Hall, Wednesday evening, at 8.30 o'clock, (Harris of Baltimore, Caterer.)

Our aim, is, primarily, to secure a large attendance of the Alumni and former Students of the College on this occasion; secondly, to have as many as possible at the Banquet, and thirdly, to receive such pecuniary assistance from the Alumni as they may be willing to contribute toward the necessary expenses of the Celebration.

Should you desire to participate in these Centennial exercises (which we strongly urge you to do,) please forward to L. D. Gassaway, Annapolis, Maryland, the sum of Three dollars ($3.00), which will entitle you to a Banquet ticket; and Two dollars ($2.00) in addition, if possible, to help to defray other expenses.

Hoping that you may find it convenient to attend, and awaiting your prompt reply,

Fraternally yours, &c.

To this circular a general and generous response was made, so that what had been deemed a probability, became an assured fact.

Invitations were sent out in the name of the Visitors and Governors of the College to many of the older and more prominent Institutions of Learning throughout the Country, to distinguished Educators, and to prominent citizens; and among the regrets received were numerous expressions of kind feelings for the College, and earnest wishes for its future success.

Baccalaureate Sermon

BY

THE RIGHT REVEREND WILLIAM PARET, D. D., LL. D.,
Bishop of Maryland, in St. Anne's Church.

ON SUNDAY MORNING the 23d of June, Members of the Faculty of St. John's, Students, and the Graduating Class in academic cap and gown, marched in procession to St. Anne's Church. A very large congregation was present.

"CHRIST, IN WHOM ARE HID ALL THE TREASURES OF WISDOM AND KNOWLEDGE."—*Colossians* ii, 3.

Is this language intended to be literal? Or is it figurative? Our answer must depend upon the true meaning of the word "Treasure." It is commonly used to express the thought of great abundance of money, jewels, precious metals and the like. And Treasuries are the places where men store and guard things of this kind, which make up what the world commonly calls wealth. Now if this be the original and true meaning of the word, then we must be speaking figuratively when we use it of things like knowledge and wisdom which have no material being.

But if a treasure, in the true meaning, be simply something valuable and precious, which from its real worth and power to help and bless, is to be prized and cherished and guarded, then its application to money and the like is only one of the specific uses of the word which has rightly a much wider range of meaning.

All things of real value, all things which from their value ought to be prized and cherished, are treasures. Shall we say that treasure is the accumulation or abundance of wealth? Take the definition; and remember as we do so, that wealth, in the derivation and careful meaning of the word, is that which can help to weal or welfare. Money and jewels and material property are wealth, only because they have power or give power to promote weal or welfare. When God by St. Paul bids every man seek not his own, but another's wealth, He does not mean another's money, but his happiness and welfare. It is then a true use of the word when we take it out of the contracted sense into which it has been suffered to fall. It means whatever can be, or be made, a possession, and gathered and guarded to promote real usefulness and welfare. The treasures of art are as truly treasures as those of gold and wisdom and knowledge; actual possessions more precious than rubies.

They are positive realities which as truly as money in any form may be sought and gained by man, and held and increased to enlarge his powers and enrich his being.

But we will not quarrel with the two uses of the word. Each helps to understand the other; and we wish to blend the meaning to-day. Let the perishing material treasure be an illustration to help us to understand the more lasting and true.

We speak then of man's gathering and accumulation of gold and property. The Bible gives the list of Solomon's possessions, and counts up his gold and silver and precious stones and ivory, exceeding all that are in the earth, for riches. And other Eastern Monarchs then and in later times laid up their enormous wealth until "the Treasures of Ind," "the riches of far Cathay," the "Oriental Magnificence," became familiar words and thoughts for the poets and other writers. Like Pharaoh they had their Treasure Cities, where in many a strong and strongly guarded room, the gold and silver were piled in enormous quantities, with the precious stones "that could not be told nor numbered for multitude." Multiply that thought ten thousand fold, and try to imagine the combined treasures of all mankind, and of all ages. Think of China, and its thousands of years of gigantic riches; India, with its many Emperors, and Persia, and Babylon and Chaldea,—and Solomon's abundance, and Egypt, and Rome, and Carthage, and Athens, and Corinth, and Ephesus, and later of Venice and Italy, and Holland, and England, and Florence, and Spain, all rich beyond reckoning. Add the almost fabulous stories of Mexico and Peru, and all that which proves them not so fabulous, the mines of California and Australia. What mind can imagine the wonder of the grand sum of such possessions, which the greed and ingenuity of man have gathered for him out of the things that were hidden in the rocks and sands of earth! The sum total of all such earthly treasures! It is beyond our power of reckoning.

Turn now to a larger measure still. .All this is but man's gathering during the little time he has lived on

earth, from the stores of such rich material upon the
earth's surface. He has only touched the outer covering. Only a few spots here and there have been opened
as mines, and in these a few hundred feet at most would
measure the depth to which such searching has gone,
and there are left untouched the massive mountains and
the solid bulk of the planet within. A million of million
times more than all that man has reached, lies yet undiscovered. These are God's treasures, God's stores; in His
treasure vaults; which He has not permitted man to
touch. What unimaginable amounts of precious things
lie stored in those thousands of miles of mystery beneath
our feet; the glittering veins and masses which human
eyes shall never see; the jewels; and the molten elements
from which God poured them forth. Shall we take a
thought wider still? This is but one of worlds innu-
merable in the seemingly boundless universe. And the
Spectroscope has told us that in those other worlds and
suns, are stored the same metallic elements, the same
material for precious things which we know here on
earth. Man with his thousands of years of hungry toiling has but gathered a drop out of the boundless oceans
of God's possessions. In God's hand are hid all these
treasures. "The Gold and the Silver are mine" He has
said; and even when man has laid his hand upon them,
God, * as He has just now so awfully shown us, can re-
claim in a moment, the souls of men, and the millions
they had toiled to gather.

Now just as really as men accumulate gold and silver,
as really do they store up and increase wisdom and
knowledge. Mind by mind, and soul by soul, each

* The disaster at Johnstown, Pa.

gathers and gains. And the combined wisdom of the individuals, communicated by interchange of thought in speech and writing and books, becomes like our imagined sum total of material wealth, an immense accumulation; a gigantic treasure.

Can you imagine it? All the studies, all the learning, all the wisdom, of all men, in all ages, from the very beginning, upon every subject which man's mind can touch? Men used to think these later ages the only wise ones. But we are looking back now with growing wonder upon the proofs of amazing knowledge in the very earliest days; in pre-historic China and Persia, and India and Egypt. Not only the beauties of their philosophic thought, but their knowledge of nature, their mathematic, and astronomic, and mechanical researches and results. There are many things in which we have gone beyond them; yet the wisest builders and thinkers of these later days must in some things bow to the minds that planned and built the pyramids. And how men in our own day have added to those stores, exploring the hidden things of nature,—the laws of power in every form, of light, of sight, of sound, of heat, of electricity, of mechanical combination, of chemical action and analysis; and how alike with gigantic strides, and with minutest microscopic study, and subtlest, and tireless effort of thought, they each day add to the world's possession of wisdom and knowledge. I thought, Brethren, that I would help you to some conception of the vastness of these mental accumulations and possessions of mankind; but it is impossible; it appals me as I get nearer to it. The vastness of all material wealth sinks into insignificance compared with it.

How immense the mere number of its subjects with which the human learning has to deal! Take some Encyclopedia and run through its alphabet of the sciences, and branches of sciences and investigation, and so count up the mines and the veins from which this precious treasure is still being gathered. What men have learned and are learning about themselves, and their own bodies and beings; some exploring the secrets of the human frame, and every limb and special organ having its own band of workers; some studying the laws and workings of the mind; some pondering the problem of the connection with the body; some studying man's soul and spiritual being; some, the mystery of what life is and in what it consists; some giving their life's work to the study of bodily disease; some to mental disease; and how out of these grow the larger studies of combined humanity; the social, national, and economic relations of men, and their history. Think what scholars have done and are doing in studying the earth on which we live. Gathering some facts, and building larger theories as to its beginning, and the times and laws and methods of its growth; the elements that constitute it; the powers at work within it,—and the laws by which they work; think of the treasures of wisdom that have been gathered in the studies of animal life, and of vegetable life. Think of the achievements in chemistry, and electricity; the wondrous wisdom of mechanical combinations and inventions; of astronomy that studies not one world, but all the millions of them, and the ties that link them together and would master the secrets of the Universe. The wisdom of mathematics, of language and its philosophy. Think of theology,—and what, by Revelation,

natural and supernatural, man has learned, and is trying
to learn concerning God, His being and nature and working, and our own relation to Him as spiritual beings.
Dear Friends, I cannot even hint to your thoughts the
thousandth part of the grand subjects, and the divisions
and sub-divisions of the labors and results of human
knowledge and wisdom. How vast and many the mines,
how countless the veins,—how maniform the material
from which the eager, tireless minds of men are bringing up to the open air of actual use the hidden truths.
How large the aim, how minute the working,—how grand
the results by which this great store of knowledge grows.

Think of the time, and there was such a time,—when
there were but ten men living upon earth, and their
almost infantile ignorance of its properties and laws, and
of the shining worlds around ; and then, taking but one
item in the long catalogue,—think how in the long ages,
fact was added to fact, and observation to observation,
and step by step man's wisdom *grew*,—till now he measures carefully the unimaginable distances which separate planets and suns, and marks out their paths, and
counts their speed to the minutest fraction of a second,—
and weighs each separate bulk, and turns the spectroscope upon the star that floats billions of miles away ;—
and tells us what are the metals and minerals and gases
that compose it. So, every branch of science has *grown*.

Gather them all together and these are the treasures
of knowledge and wisdom which man has gathered.

The grand libraries of the world are treasure cities,
where in countless manuscripts and printed books such
gathered wealth is stored. The Halls of learning, like
this venerable College, and the great universities are

workshops, where it is fashioned into fresh forms and combinations,—the mints which turn the solid ingots into current coin. And from mind to mind,—from brain to brain, it passes in exchange and use. And faster than the gold and silver flowing in from our far West, and from Australia, the tide of increasing knowledge pours in every day. Among all the wonders of the human race, its achievements in accumulated wisdom and knowledge, are by far the most amazing.

And yet, dear friends, this too, is but the scratching of the surface. Like the miles upon miles of the solid unsearched earth beneath us ; like the gathered bulk of the countless, mysterious worlds of far-reaching space, is the measureless wealth of truth and truths as yet unreached, undreamed of, by human intellect.

One of the greatest of living searchers and gatherers,— perhaps the leader of the world in natural science, has expressed under another figure what I am trying to speak ; he writes, that with all that man has learned, and with all that ages and human study may yet accomplish, we stand upon the shore of a boundless ocean of truth unknown and hid in mystery, across which the mere human mind may never hope to pass.

Alas! that the littleness of human knowledge and capacity which he thus declares, has not made him more reverent and humble in thinking and speaking of the things which may be possible to power and intellect divine !

For all these things still hidden from man, are, like gold and silver yet buried in the deep heart of the earth, actually existent in the sight and knowledge of God.

Before man found the gold, it was there ; and all that he has failed to find, is as real as what his eyes have seen. Before man found it, God made it,—gathered the elements of its being, watched its growth, fixed the laws of its distribution, and knew where every grain of it was hidden.

Before man discovers what he calls a new truth, that truth was in existence, was a fact, and was clear to that infinite and divine intellect, from which nothing is hid. Age had passed upon age, before the mind of man conceived what has been called the law of gravity;—but through all those ages,—the force or law of which we thus speak was unceasingly measuring the places and movements of all worlds, and of every atom in each. Ages upon ages passed before man dreamed of the wonders that in our own day have flashed into human knowledge and use in the mysteries of electric force, but all these,—and the still unimaginable things which may be hereafter discovered,—were as real from the beginning as they are to-day. Though man should yet live on earth for years unending, and his work in gathering wisdom's yet hidden treasures, should go on with ever-accelerated swiftness beyond the present marvellous rate, he will, at his wisest, still be blundering and guessing at the very threshold of what has forever been grasped by One Intellect absolutely.

Well may St. Paul cry out "Oh, the depth of the wisdom and knowledge of God." Man's mightiest achievements are but the surface scratching. "In Him are hid all the treasures of wisdom and knowledge."

If I have at all succeeded in my effort to show the real meaning of the words of my text,—may I have your patience for a very few words concerning its use.

And first one or two things which I can merely suggest, for your thought. They are far too large for our full study now. Had it been written that "In God are hid all the treasures of wisdom and knowledge" it would have seemed but natural and right that to the Infinite Deity,—the infinite and absolute mastership and possession of all intellect and intellectual power should belong. When then the word is not "God" but "Christ,"—"Christ in whom are hid all the treasures of wisdom and knowledge," that simple sentence becomes one of the grandest and most absolute declarations that Christ is God. It did not *intend* to assert Christ's divinity. That was not a point in the thought at the time.

But all the more powerfully, because of its unintendedness, it does declare His divinity. St. Paul knew that great truth. His mind had no room for question about it,—and so with the full force of unhesitating acceptance, he simply asserts as belonging to Christ, the absolute infiniteness of knowledge which can belong to none but God. But that Christ was also a man ; and we think of the Child Jesus ; the village carpenter at Nazareth ; the gentle, patient man,—who from the humble earthly home went forth to teach men, to bless them, to bear their misunderstandings, their contempt, their hatred, their cruelties. And grand as that life seemed to me before—it seems far grander now, as I remember that "in Him are hid all the treasures of wisdom and knowledge." Marvellous His words seemed before. Simple, direct, unpretending, unboastful,—but with a power and possession of truth, in which all the ages have found no room for error. I remember how He said when speaking of the things of Heaven, "We speak that we do know." And in Him alone of all who ever walked the earth, was there never a thought or word that could conflict with St. Peter's loving Confession : "Thou knowest all things." But how amazing in its tenderness is the condescension that brought that absoluteness of infinite knowledge thus into the simple every day conversations and relations of human life. How wondrous the love, thus to bring down that infinite intellect, to walk for awhile in the narrow ways of man's scanty comprehension !

These, Brethren, are my suggestions. And now for my last.

The infiniteness of intellectual possibilities ; the infiniteness of the facts and relations and workings of the mind ; the reality of these treasures of wisdom and knowledge, are a proof of the mighty intellect that called them into being. If the order and power of the material world compel the thought of an infinite power, the order and wonderful beauties of a world of intellect, compel the confession of an infinite understanding. It is a wonder to me that any man could be an atheist who studies the human body, or the nature of material things. But a hundred fold more wonderful that any man can be a student of the mind and its workings, and its combinations and powers and possessions, and deny the being of a God. Sad indeed, and ruinous, is the pride of intellect which sometimes takes that direction. Thank God, that the annals of human learning show almost all of its great names in the past, among the believers in God and Christ. Thank God that among the wondrous scholars of our own memory, and of this present time, with very few exceptions, the noblest and best have not weakened the vigor, nor fettered the freedom of their thought, but rather ennobled it and given it grander range by inspiring it with a reverent belief in God and love for Christ and His wisdom and love.

The "Agnostic" claims indeed to be freed from fetters, because he casts off religion. But in reality, he is binding fetters on himself, by thus limiting to things of material sense, or of which his own imperfect intellect may be the test and measure, the powers of mind and soul which God means to reach out to things invisible and eternal. God has opened two worlds to human thought. The Agnostic repudiates one of them, and dwarfs his being in so doing.

Oh, scholars,—learners,—seekers for wisdom and knowledge,—whether in the path of special investigations, the finding and bringing up of truths yet unknown; or those who, as in this College, labor in learning and teaching, and storing up and using the wisdom already gained,— let the grand lesson of our text teach us the scholar's true humility ; to recognize not in word only, but in deepest conscience, man's narrow range and abounding error; to remember that however he may err, or how little he may reach, there is such a thing as truth infallible,—and that the Lordship of that belongs to the Lord Jesus Christ.

Thank God that from this institution in the hundred years of its work for which we now rejoice,—it has sent forth its bands of scholars, trained not to be doubters, but believers, by the power of an education in which Christian faith and reverence and docility were felt to be not hindrances and frailties, but stepping stones to grander reach of mind and soul! We know not what fortunes yet await the labors here. But God grant that whatever course they take, St. John's College may be true to its name, as a place of Christian learning; a bulwark against that narrow and hardening school of Science which will own no science save in material things. There are wonders undiscovered on earth and planets and suns, which make of man's grandest accomplishments only puny child's play. There are wonders in spiritual being and intelligent life beyond the range of this human race, grander orders of life and thought; and almost infinite are the truths concerning us, that are as much unknown as the spaces which lie beyond the outermost recognized star. But there is an eye that looks all through those far far regions of space unexplored, and an intellect to which every truth or relation or possibility of the Universe is clear as the noon-day, and that is "Christ, in whom are hid all the treasures of wisdom and knowledge."

On SUNDAY EVENING, the 23d of June, the REVEREND VAUGHAN S. COLLINS, A. M. in Salem Methodist Episcopal Church, delivered a Sermon before the Young Men's Christian Association of St. John's College, in the presence of a large audience, including Members of the Faculty and many Students. .

Sermon.

BY

THE REVEREND VAUGHAN S. COLLINS, A. M.,
Pastor of Scott Methodist Episcopal Church, Wilmington, Delaware.

BEHOLD, THE FEAR OF THE LORD, THAT IS WISDOM; AND TO DEPART FROM EVIL IS UNDERSTANDING.—*Job* xxviii. 28.

The work of the Young Men's Christian Association in College is my theme.

There is a demand in our day as never before in the history of the world for education; but this to be most effective must develope man in his three-fold nature. It is a matter of daily experience that a man may be developed or educated on one side of his nature and not on another. He may be developed physically until his body becomes the nicest of machines; but that may be all, he knows nothing else, is fitted for nothing else. How often we hear the remark "He is a fine mechanic; but he is good for nothing else." That means the man has been well educated physically—his eye and hand have been very thoroughly trained; yet, in intellect he may be a babe, and in morals a demon.

So, too, we find men educated intellectually. Their heads are full of scientific and literary lore. They "understand all mysteries and all knowledge." Yet, all that intellect is carted around in a little, weazened, half dead body; and their moral nature is as little developed as their physical. They are book-worms, nothing more. They can tell you the date of the battle of Arbela or the fall of Babylon, but not the date when the gas bill is due. They can tell you all about the history of the Pyramids, or the formation of the Macedonian phalanx, or the Eleusinian mysteries; but not mysteries of making a livelihood, or of buying beef and vegetables. These are intellectual men—intellect gone to seed. Then you will find men educated spiritually, or religiously, but undeveloped along the other two sides of their nature. These are right at home on religious matters. They can read prayers like a priest, or sing, or give good advice, and love God and men most sincerely; and if they should die would go straight home to heaven; yet they may be very poor mechanics, miserable merchants, failures in business matters. In physique and mind they may be very much dwarfed and distorted.

It is evident such education makes one-sided men; for the education is one-sided. It is also apparent that the ideal man has all three of these diverse natures of his developed or educated to their highest capabilities.

The ideal education is that which tends to develope this ideal man. It should be the aim of all our colleges to afford opportunities for this complex or composite education.

I. PHYSICAL EDUCATION.

Any system that loses sight of the fact that man is primarily and essentially an animal is built upon a false foundation. We are animals—animal bodies, animal appetites, animal propensions, animal functions; and we will have these as long as we are in the body. However much the intellectual man may scorn this so-called "lower part" of his being; and the religious enthusiast may rant about the "prison house of clay;" and seek by fasting and penance self-imposed, to macerate and maim the body, that the spiritual nature may shine forth more clearly through the rents made in the earthly casket; the fact still remains that we are animals, and as such have animal wants. The animal life begins before the intellectual and spiritual life awake. So education should primarily be physical education. From earliest childhood the laws of health should be taught, and their demands made imperative. Let the child understand that they can never be the model man or woman unless they have the model body for the model mind and model spirit to dwell in. Let them be taught that lily fingers and wasp waists are never to be purchased at the price of soft muscles and cramped viscera. It is a sign of better days when our colleges are awaking to this subject of athletics all over the land, and encouraging the students, and in some even compelling the students to take part. A college is not worthy of the name that does not provide apparatus and instruction to develope its students to the highest degree of physical perfection consistent with health. Let the student be constantly impressed with the fact that he who goes forth from the college with a diseased, or half developed body, no matter how full his head may be, will have a terrible struggle to keep up with his brother of more brawn, if, perhaps, with a few less Greek roots in his head.

The body, however, is not the chief thing to receive attention in college; it is only one of the co-ordinates of importance. The college is not organized for the purpose of turning out champion base-ballists or oars-men, or developing professional pugilists or pedestrians. The student whose highest ambition is to be the best athlete in the school, or to win the captaincy of the ball team or boating crew, has a very low ideal as to what the college may be to him.

The most prominent feature of our colleges usually is

,II. MENTAL TRAINING.

This I would call higher education, not in contradistinction from the education of the lower grade schools, as is usual; but in contrast with the physical, which is the positive, or primary education.

The multitudinous helps afforded by the college for mental developement might be grouped under three heads: the mingling with professors, as superiors in learning, with students as equals, and the opportunity of reading good books under the wise guidance of master minds.

The youth often comes to college with very exalted ideas of his mental attainments. Father and mother have told him so often how smart he is; obliging neighbors have so frequently pointed him out as the brightest young man in the neighborhood; and finally the village school master has acknowledged that he can teach no more—the boy has learned all he knows and more too; these combined so inflate the young man that by the time his clothes are packed for college he finds his hat three sizes too small for his head. *He knows it*

all. But when he reaches college, a wise looking doctor
of science, or doctor of philosophy, or doctor of divinity,
or doctor of laws, or doctor of some real or imaginary
something—when this wise looking doctor, with his gold
glasses, and shiny bald head, and fierce mustache or
shaggy beard, takes that youth into a gloomy, dingy
room, (that has not been aired all summer,) hands him
a catalogue, points out his own name, and motions him
to be seated.   The youth reads, "J. Solomon Wiseman,
A. B., A. M., Ph. D., D. D., LL. D., L. H. D., S. T.
D., A. R. S. S., Professor of Ancient and Modern Languages, Lecturer Royal to the University Antique."
He begins to look from the professor to the catalogue,
and from the catalogue to the professor; and every time
he looks he sees more to wonder and admire.   He now
finds his head much too small for his hat.   What he
thought he knew before coming to college he now finds
rapidly oozing from his boot-soles or evaporating from
his brain.   Presently, when he can speak, he faintly asks,
pointing to the many titled name in the catalogue,
"Is that you?"   The professor coldly replies, "Est,
Quid rogas?"   The poor youth's heart fails, perspiration
breaks out all over him, and he gasps to think he is in
the presence of such surpassing wisdom.

That first interview is generally sufficient to knock
the self-conceit out of the newcomer; but if he should
have a relapse, the sophomores have an infallible remedy
they will be only too happy to apply.

Exaggeration aside, this contact with learned men is
a vast help to a young man seeking truth and mental
ripeness.   These professors have passed through the

same troubles of mind, of perplexing doubt, of mental darkness and uncertainty, in which the student so often finds himself; and to have a learned, level headed friend to whom you may go at any time to have doubts removed, and find guidance in one's search for truth, is a boon of inestimable value. Were I speaking to professors instead of to students, I would say, every professor, to fill his position properly, must be a Christian ; and a professor, who is approachable in the class room *only*, is a poor substitute for a teacher. The sooner he seeks elsewhere for a situation the better for college and students.

The contact with students is also wonderfully stimulating and helpful. It is difficult, if not impossible, to get community of interest anywhere to such an extent as among students of the same college. Young men of the most active period of life, living together, studying the same books, eating at the same table, sharing the same labors, the same sports, day after day, week after week, for three or four years—no wonder college boys always have been and always will be clannish. In college, as no where else on earth, a young man is most accurately measured as to what he really is. In the world it depends to quite a degree as to how much money your father has, or who your grand-father was, whether you will have friends or not. No matter what you do, before the world will applaud it will stop to ask, "Who is that fellow?" Not so with college boys. No matter who your father is, if you are a dunce they will not be long in telling you so. No matter how many sweet, pet names your mother may call you, if you are a coward and a sneak, the boys do not hesitate to brand you by

the true name. College boys are the truest democrats—
they believe in every boy having a fair chance. They
are also the truest aristocrats—they believe in letting
the best man have first place. You can not pass a
counterfeit on college boys. They hate shams; but no
matter from what humble surroundings a new man may
come, if he proves himself a good, true, honest man the
college boys will rally round and stand by him. I sometimes think it is worth the time and cost of a course at
college to get one's proper rating.

Then comes the benefit of books. Our college libraries are Wisdom's banquet rooms, spread with all the
dainties the Goddess can provide, with doors wide open
to all students, and over the entrance the word "WEL-
COME!" What treasures of priceless worth are stored
upon those shelves! What jewels rare, of mind and
heart, lie hidden within those coverings of skin and
cloth! Student, you are greatly wronging yourself if
you fail to work this mine of mental wealth. The library
is the great improvement of the modern over the university of the middle ages. Then if a student would learn
he must go to the living teacher. Books were more
costly than a journey to the place where the lecturer
taught. Hungering for light and knowledge, without
books to satisfy the craving, I am not surprised that
thirty thousand students from all parts of Europe flocked
to Paris to learn of Abelard; and ten thousand were studying law one year at Bologna.

Suppose then you educate the physique of the young
man to its highest possible development—until every
muscle, sinew, bone and nerve is in most perfect con-

dition of power and sensibility. Then suppose you have at the same time trained his mind, until by means of professors, students, and books he is cultured to the highest possible degree—filled with the love of the past and the science and men of to-day. What then? Have you benefited the young man? No, you have cursed him if you stop there. Physical and mental culture a curse? Yes, a curse if you stop there. I know grim old Carlyle says, that if the devil should ask him the way to the school house, he would point him the way; for he would be less a devil by learning geography and philosophy. I say such talk is nonsense. To educate the devil would be to make him a still worse devil, a devil of increased power for evil, unless his nature be changed.

Let me illustrate. A youth of eighteen years is noticed to be uncommonly strong. He can lift more, can carry more than any man in the shops. He is taken from the shops and physically educated until he is called an Adonis, a model of physical perfection,—his eye like that of an eagle, his hand as quick as the kitten and strong as the tiger. But your training has transformed an honest shop-boy into a champion prize-fighter, who now starts out to prove he can whip any man in the world; and so fond of fighting is he, that if he can find no one else to fight, he goes home to beat his wife until she is compelled to leave him. Has not your physical education cursed that young man?

Take another case. Here is a man who is a marvel in iron work. His especial delight is in making fine tools. He can temper a chisel that will cut anything that needs cutting, or a drill that will bore into the hardest chilled steel like wood. He is justly proud of his skill, gets good wages, and is content. That man gets a little mental education. As his mind expands he begins to think beyond the four walls of his shop. He gets to think that his skill would be better paid in breaking safes than in making them. He becomes a bank burglar. Ask him as he lies in prison to day, if his mental education was not a curse to him.

It is the same in more purely mental culture. What do I care if a man knows all there is to be known, and can pour out his knowledge in silver streams of polished eloquence, glittering with jewels of wit and adorned with the beauties of rhetoric—what care I for all these if from his mouth there comes the *false* instead of the true? What difference if he knows all about the Phœnicians and Assyrians, if he will not pay his debts?

Suppose you determine to build a locomotive that shall surpass in speed and power anything yet built. You cast the drive wheels twenty feet high. You build the boiler a hundred feet long, and strong enough to bear a thousand pounds to the square inch. Everything else is on the same gigantic scale. You have calculated that engine will pull twenty loaded passenger cars one hundred and fifty miles an hour. It is all finished. You bring a skilled engineer to give his opinion. He looks at the lofty smoke-stack and immense boiler with a smile of satisfaction. Examines the mammoth steam chests and cylinders and pistons with increasing delight. His face glows with honest pride as he thinks he is to mount the engineer's perch and handle that mighty throttle. He looks at the drive wheels and a cloud comes over his

face. He peers into the cab and the cloud deepens.
"What is the matter?" you ask. "Well, sir, your
engine is very pretty, but it is good for nothing. It is
big enough, and pretty enough, and powerful enough to
do all you expect it to do; but it has neither flanges on the
drive wheels, reverse bar, nor brakes. Without flanges
you can not keep it on the track; and without reverse
bar and brakes you could never stop the thing if once it
got to going. I would not ride on it a half mile if you
would give it to me."

This is what you have done with a man if you stop
his education with his body and mind; you have built
a beautiful machine of tremendously increased power;
but an unmanageable, uncertain thing that you can not
depend upon keeping the track. An engine that will
jump the track is only more dangerous at every increase
of power you give it; and so it is with man. A fearful
thing it is to see a locomotive leap from the rails and
dash down an embankment dragging behind it cars
loaded with human beings. Infinitely worse is it to
see a bright, vigorous man off the track, dashing downward toward the bottomless pit, dragging behind him a
host of friends who regarded him as a model. It is a
fine thing to increase the calibre of your guns and the
weight of ball they will carry; but is it so fine if the
heavier artillery is to be turned against you? Do you
not value a rifle ball fired *for* you, more than a hundred
ton cannon ball fired *against* you? Increase the calibre
and power as much as you will, but be sure the gun
will shoot for us.

Here is a lawyer of masterly intellect, and wonderful
eloquence. What a power he might be for justice and

the right! But he bends every energy of his great mind
to defeat justice and shield crime. Would it not be better if, like Samson, his locks were shorn? Here is a
physician of wondrous skill. How much he might do to
alleviate suffering! . He, however, stoops to use all his
skill in the aid of secret vice. Would it not have been
manifold better if he had never learned the use of medicine? Here is a preacher, who uses all his powers of
analytical skill to overthrow the very doctrines he had
vowed to sustain. He was polished that he might shine
among the giants of the Lord; but all his powers of eloquent denunciation he ranges against those he was pledged
to assist; and fights against the only light that tends to
drive the darkness from this dark world. Were it not
better had he never received this higher training?

Something then is needed to keep the man on the track
—something that shall guide him in the right path.
What is that something? It is the highest form of education, it is

III. SOUL EDUCATION; RELIGION, if you please.

The Master said: "Seek ye first the kingdom of God,
and His righteousness; and all. these things shall be
added unto you." The text declares: "Behold, the
fear of the Lord that is wisdom; and to depart from evil
is understanding."

This is the highest form of education, it is the essential part of education. This grade of culture, and this
only, will fit a man for greatest happiness for himself;
and this means, making him most serviceable to others.
It matters not so much what a man is physically or men-

tally; but the all-important question is, what is he spiritually? Education to be complete must develope character, and the right kind of character. The model is sketched by divine inspiration in 2 Peter, i. 5-7: "Add to your faith virtue; and to virtue knowledge; and to knowledge temperance; and to temperance patience; and to patience godliness; and to godliness brotherly kindness; and to brotherly kindness charity."

Here is your model man. He believes in God as the very foundation stone of his whole character. He not only has living faith in God, but he has virtue, true manliness. He is a manly man, honest, brave and true. Not this only, for he has knowledge—a cultured mind stored with learning of men and wisdom of God. He is also temperate—in eating, in drinking, in his words, in his acts; temperate, not rash. In him we find the charming grace of patience; not brusque, nor peevish, nor cross; but able to bear the ills of life with quiet, cheerful spirit, without showing teeth and claws. He is also one who takes God for his life example—he seeks godliness, god-like-ness. He endeavors to think the thoughts of God, to do the acts of God, to live the life his God would live. Yet, while thus communing with the great Jehovah, he never forgets that about him are the weak and sinful. It is easy to love a being of infinite tenderness and goodwill like our God; but it takes a deal of grace to love poor, erring, sinning men all about us. This model man is equal to the task. He shows kindness to his brethren, whether of family, church or society. His kindness flows from a heart warm with love for his brethren. Nor is it all. A man may love those of his own blood, or those with whom he daily mingles; and yet be far from loving those who are not congenial in tastes, doctrines or manners. This model man is able to take this last step in the ascending scale, and reaches the higher plane of charity, love for all men. He can reach up to those above him in wealth and rank without feeling envy, and reach down to the lowest in life or rank without feeling pride. Here we have the type of manhood to which we should all aspire.

Now, what part of the college curriculum is especially adapted to develope that kind of man? Shall it be referred to the classical department? It is not there especially taught. To the mathematical? The professor will tell you he is paid to teach mathematics, not creeds and religion. Will the department of natural science furnish the kind of spiritual education needed to develope such a man? No; their's is the realm of matter, not spirit. Do you say the churches are to furnish such education? The churches can do little unless the college be a denominational one. If it be a denominational college of course the church of that denomination will see to the spiritual instruction of the students; but if it be a state institution or a non-sectarian college the case is different. Having no church establishment in this country, a state or non-sectarian college is virtually beyond the reach of all the churches, *as such*. A non-sectarian college should be one in which all the denominations patronizing it should have systematic spiritual services and instruction in regular succession, alternating with each other. Such services should be free from all denominational bias and peculiarities; and the instruction should be free from all denominational cant. But unless such regular work is systematically carried on, in which all the denominations share equally and honorably, what then?

Then no denomination is at liberty to enter the college precincts with its own sectarian way. The Methodists have no more right to hold a service that is purely Methodistic than the Roman Catholics have to celebrate the Mass. The Presbyterians have no more right to preach Calvinism, nor the Baptists to have an immersion service in college, than the Protestant Episcopalians would have to teach apostolic succession, or to coach candidates for confirmation. The churches then, *as such*, have no authority to enter the college precincts even upon their holy mission. To allow all denominations to enter and teach their peculiar views would cause endless confusion. To allow any one to enter upon such a mission is not only denominational discourtesy, but it is not fair play. Denominational lines must cease at the entrance to the campus. Inside all must be individual Christians only.

Then how shall this part of one's education, the highest, the most important part, be taught? By the Young Men's Christian Association of the college. This is their special work; and if not done by them it will not be done at all. The young men who join this organization are Christians of all the denominations in the college. Here they stand upon the same platform, irrespective of churchly ties. It is their duty to hold up this Bible standard of manhood by every means in their power—teaching it by word and living example. To do this most effectually they must seek to arouse an interest in the study of the Bible, and faith in its teachings.

It seems a strange anomaly that in this so-called Christian land so few of the colleges have any place in their curriculum for the study of this book of books, the Bible. If the history of our country teaches us anything it is that the Bible is the rock on which our civil and religious institutions are founded. Our fathers believed in the Bible, claimed the God of the Bible as their God; appealed to Him in hours of darkness for help, and in their brighter hours praised Him for the help afforded. Besides, the very name of the book shows its importance. In all languages and by all peoples it is called "the Bible," "The Book." Christian and infidel, pagan, saint, and sinner all call it "*the Book;*" thus testifying that it is "*the Book*" of prime importance. Yet, it is a sad fact, that many of our college students are graduated who have less knowledge of the Bible than almost any book in polite literature. They have spent a year in studying the manners and customs of the Romans, and another year on those of the Greeks; but they have never spent an hour in studying the history of that people who were chosen of God to keep alive true knowledge of Him. Caesar and Seneca, Pericles and Socrates they know; but they know not Noah and Abraham, Jacob and Elijah. They are taught to appreciate the beauties and musical rhythm of Homer and Sophocles; but not a word said of those grand lyrics of David, the glowing imagery of Isaiah, or the weird grandeur of the Apocalypse. The laws of Draco and Lycurgus must be mastered; while the laws of Moses are not discussed in English, much less translated from the original. They must wade through the slums of Rome with Juvenal, and be familiar with Scott and Shakspeare and

3

Dryden, or they can not get their diploma; but they may never have heard of the New Jerusalem and its glories, nor of Paul, nor of Stephen, nor of Jesus of Nazareth, and yet they are allowed to lead their class. The consequence is that many young men who come to college Christians, or at least believers in God and the Bible, during their four years course hear them so seldom mentioned, and then, perhaps, only to be criticized for imaginary mistakes, that they come to regard the Bible as only good to supply mothers with nursery stories; but for full grown men it is behind the times. All this because he has not been trained in Bible lore as he has in scientific and classical lore. In science, art, and history he has been developed from the boy to the man; but in the Bible he remains the same ignorant child; and as these learned men about them seem to care little or nothing about these things, the student learns to regard the Bible and religion in much the same light as the Arabian Nights and the hobgoblin stories of childhood.

What would a learned Hindoo think, coming from his land where their holy books form such an important part of the curriculum in their schools—what would he think when he found our holy book was not taught at all nor recognized as any part of the course of study necessary to a Christian education? What would a cultured Arab think, who had been compelled to pore over the Koran so long before he was regarded as educated; what would he think on visiting scores of our principal colleges, to find that in *Christian* education Christ and His word formed no part? Is it not a shame on us as Christians that these things are so?

Here, then, is a great work for the Young Men's Christian Association of every college in the land; to do all they can to have the Bible systematically taught in their colleges, just as other branches of learning are taught. Petition the faculty and trustees to provide means that you may be taught, yea, thoroughly taught the heavenly wisdom of this most wonderful book. I am glad to note the wide-spread interest exhibited by some of our colleges along this line of study. May God hasten the day when the Bible shall have a foremost place in every curriculum!

Do you ask why I am so much in earnest about this? Because the Bible is "THE BOOK" in *fact*, as well as in name. There are three questions that are of most vital importance to every human being: Whence am I? What am I? Whither am I going? To these three questions the Bible, and the Bible only, furnishes a reasonable answer.

I. THE BIBLE GIVES US THE ONLY REASONABLE ORIGIN OF MAN.

No doubt some of you may think I am now treading on dangerous ground. I want to be understood as saying that the origin of man as given in Genesis stands on a more secure footing to-day, than it has ever stood. There has been quite a stir in both. theological and scientific circles about the first three chapters of Genesis. Within the present century there has been some pretty loud bragging as to the havoc scientific knowledge was about to make with our Bible account of creation. Many learned theologians seemed to lose heart, and hastened to meet the so-called new scientists to arrange terms of capitulation, lest the Bible should come off defeated. What is the result? The battle has been fought, the smoke is lifting, the débris is being cleared away, and we find that *there is no contradiction between science and revelation; they are parts of one whole.* The newest revelations of science only strengthen the bulwarks of our Zion, and lead to a clearer knowledge of what the Bible really does teach.

There are two explanations or accounts of creation, and only two, that receive any special attention by the thinking men of to-day, the materialistic and the biblical. Both of these are evolution theories. An outline of the two may aid you in seeing just how the matter stands.

There are many various shades of doctrines among the materialistic evolutionists; in fact it is difficult to find two who agree; but in the main their theory may be sketched thus:

They start with a universe of matter; for matter with them is eternal. This universe of homogeneous, chaotic matter somehow, during the lapse of ages, manages to resolve itself into the various forms of solid, liquid, and gaseous. Ages pass, and this dead matter learns how to transform itself into living matter, or protoplasm. This protoplasm, or bioplasm (both are used interchangeably), which is only the simplest form of a vegetable cell, somehow, after untold ages transforms itself into various grades of vegetable life. Another era of ages passes, and it determines it will change itself into an animal; and so it does. Beginning with the protozoans, it gets more and more ambitious until it changes itself into a radiate, then an articulate, then into a vertebrate; and then, after running the whole gamut of the vertebrates, finally becomes man, the king of creation. So beginning with dead matter, a universe of it, these wise men can build us the entire universe, even up to man. On what is the whole theory founded? On the imagination of its authors! The very facts of science, of which they so fondly boast, are all against them. No scientific investigator has ever been found who says he has discovered how dead matter becomes living substance. After years of anxious watching and most careful observation over large portions of the earth's surface, no one has ever found where one species of animal ever changed itself into another species. Even Haekel, the noted German says, "Spontaneous generation is a thing that never yet has been demonstrated; but it must be accepted, or we shall have to adopt a miracle to bring about the necessary transformation." Precisely; and that is just what the Christian scientist does.

Compare this hypothetical account of creation with the Bible account. Instead of starting with the universe of dead matter it starts with an omnipotent, omniscient being who is called God. He is a free, voluntary agent distinct from His work. By His inherent power He fashions the heavens and the earth according to His will. His creation is marked by three distinct periods. He first creates matter. When that is created He proceeds to fashion it; dividing the heavens from the earth, the sea from the land, and causes flowers and grass and trees to grow. The second great creation is when He makes living animals—a new creation here separate and distinct from anything yet made. This word "create"

shows that God in "creating" animals put something
new in the universe; something not in matter, not even in
organized matter, for plants were organized. Then for
the third time that word "*bara*," "create," comes in, in
reference to the creation of man. "God created (*bara*)
man in His own image; in His own image created (*bara*)
He them; male and female created (*bara*) He them."

Here is an account of creation which is not only vouched
for the inspiration of God as Christians believe; which
has the support of tradition of that peculiar people,
the Jews; which agrees in the main with the accounts
of the most primitive peoples, as "the Chaldeans, the
Phoenicians, the Egyptians, the Persians, the Indians,
the Chinese, the Karens, the Greeks, the Romans, the
Celts, the Scandinavians, the Finlanders, the Peruvians,
the Aztecs, the Algonquins, &c.;" and besides all this
cumulative traditionary testimony, is confirmed by most
persistent scientific research. The same order of succession given in Genesis is the order of succession given by
geology. Here is progression, here is evolution. Not
the blind evolution of dead matter; but evolution with
a sentient evolver, who knows He wants to do, and does
it. When He desired the "wastiness and emptiness"
of chaos to be filled with matter He calls it into being.
When He wants that disordered matter to assume shape
He speaks, and it is done. When he wants that inor-
ganic matter to organize into vegetable life He organizes
it. When He wants animals to move on land, and fishes
to swim the sea, and birds to fly in the air, He speaks
and they "swarm with swarms." When at last everything was all ready for him for whom He has prepared it,

He fashions man's body of the earth, and breathes into his nostrils the breath of lives, and man becomes a living soul.

The one system makes man a child of the clod, nothing more; the other says," "He is not only child of the clod, but also the child of God. The one system ascribes to every grain of sand, every drop of water, every mote in the atmosphere, all the eternity, wisdom and power that we ascribe to God. Verily, they have "Lords many, and Gods many." Now which seems to you the more reasonable origin of man: that of a few men calling themselves scientists, yet who on their own admission have failed to find a single scientific fact on which to base their theory; who grant all this power and wisdom to dead matter, and bow down and worship matter as their creator; or, that of the Bible, which has not only the traditional and intrinsic truth of its own inspired record, but the cosmogonies of other nations, and all the observations of science to confirm the truth of its statements? Which will you claim for your ancestry: the ape for your father, the tadpole for your grandfather, and the clod of the earth for your creator; or, will you claim the God-made Adam for your father, Jesus of Nazareth for your brother, and the God of heaven for your creator? Give me the divine record, with its ennobling, exalting inspirations, arising from our divine parentage.

The Bible should claim our thought because

II. It, only, tells us what we now are.

The Psalmist but voiced the soul of humanity, of heathen, infidel, pagan and Christian when he asked, "What

is man?" There is no book in the world but the Bible
that can answer that question. Read science, and you
find man is an animal. Read of industry and art, and
you conclude man is a working animal. Read philology,
and man is a talking animal. Read history, and man is
a fighting animal. Read philosophy, and man is a thinking animal. Read poetry and romance, and man is a loving animal. Read theology, and man is a worshipping
animal. So you may travel the entire circle of human
learning and you find man an animal. That is as far as
human wisdom unaided has gone or can go. But what
you have thus found by ranging the entire field of literature you could have read in this one book, the Bible.
More than that: the Bible alone tells of that part, or nature
of man, which is not animal. I know I am of the earth,
earthy; but I am conscious of inner aspirations that are
not earthy. Whence these longings for higher and better
and holier living? Whence this craving for more light,
more wisdom? Yet how is it that in the same man there
are low, base desires and appetites? How is it that to-day
man is pursuing the noble, the lofty, the pure, the good,
striving to fashion himself according to the divine pattern;
and to-morrow, that same man is just as vigorously engaged in things that debase, debauch, and destroy? Yea,
how is it that at the *same moment* in the same breast there
is found a desire to do the right and true, and a counter
desire to do the wrong and base?

The Bible explains this. Man was created in the image
of his maker; which consisted of "righteousness and true
holiness." So while man was an animal in body and
soul, in spirit (πνεῦμα) he was like his God. This divine

element or nature was designed to rule the man; and it did rule until man sinned. When Adam sinned he lost this image of God. His πνεῦμα, or spiritual nature lost its grip on the σῶμα and ψῦχή. The latter ruled instead of the former. That which was designed to be master was now servant. This was the death that came upon Adam. His body did not die, his animal ψῦχή did not die; but his πνεῦμα separated from God by sin, was no more its former self than the dead man is like the live one.

This accounts for that war within us, which Saint Paul so clearly yet pathetically describes in Romans VII. "For that which I do I allow not: for what I would, that do I not; but what I hate, that do I. * * * For the good that I would I do not; but the evil which I would not, that I do. * * * For I delight in the law of God after the inward man: but I see another law in my members, warring against the law of my mind, and bringing me into captivity to the law of sin which is in my members." Every thoughtful man must acknowledge that the apostle has here portrayed an internal experience common to mankind. Our lives are not what we desire them to be. They are not what God intended them to be, nor what that of Adam was before the fall. How then shall that higher life be regained, the life in which the πνεῦμα reigns, and the ψῦχή is brought into subjection? Only by a spiritual agony, struggle, change, called regeneration. The Master told Nicodemus "Verily, verily, I say unto you, Ye must be born again." No wonder Nicodemus replied, "How can a man be born when he is old?" For in this great change in which the Bible says the "old man" dies and we become "new creatures," literally "a. new creation," what in man is so completely changed as to merit such strong terms? Not his body; that remains the same. Not his ψῡχή animal life or soul; that remains the same. Then what is changed, or added to him, or taken from him that is worthy of being called a new birth? It is the resurrection of this dead πνεῡμα, this essence of divinity given him at creation and lost through the fall; and not a resurrection merely, but a placing it on the throne of the man's mind, will, and affections. The reign of the usurping ψῡχή is ended, and the reign of the πνεῡμα begins. This is new life, yea the only true, full life for man. This is what the Master meant when He said, "I am come that ye might have life; and that ye might have it more abundantly." Young men, seek this higher life!

Again, the pre-eminence of the Bible is shown in the fact that

III. It alone teaches man's destiny.

It is said of Buddha, that when quite a young man, he was walking through the princely gardens when he met a funeral procession. On the bier lay the wrapped corpse of an infant; and behind the bier followed the young father and mother, bemoaning the loss of their first born. The great heart of Buddha was touched. He withdrew to his private chamber and meditated upon what he had seen. "Is this life? to be cut off in infancy, like a tender bud, before the petals have been allowed to bloom? To kill the nestling before it has tried its wings? To quench the fire before the flame is kindled." And he pondered these things in his heart.

Again Buddha goes forth for a walk amid the trees of the garden; and lō, another funeral procession! This time the corpse is that of a beautiful young bride; and following the bier is her handsome young husband wailing with breaking heart the anguish that is crushing him. And Buddha retires to his private chamber to meditate. "Is this life? To be allowed to reach full age only to be cut off? To be offered the cup of joy only to have it dashed from our hand as we raise it to our lips?" And Buddha pondered these things in his heart.

For the third time Buddha goes forth for a walk amid the trees of the garden; and lō, for the third time a funeral procession! This time upon the bier lies the form of an old man, wrinkled with age, his scattering locks frosted with the snows of many years; and no mourners follow the bier. And again Buddha retires for meditation: "Is this life? To live on, while wife and children die? To live on, until friends are dead? To live on, until unknown and unloved, stranger hands must bear us to the tomb?" And with soul darkened by what his eyes had seen Buddha goes forth to preach "Life is a burdensome curse."

I am not surprised. In my pastoral work I see so much of suffering, so much of sorrow, so much of innocence suffering for the guilty, so much of weakness oppressed by strength, so much of poverty ground down by wealth, so much of the good persecuted by the bad, that my heart grows sick within me. I can but ask myself "Is this life? to labor, and toil, and suffer for three score years and ten, and then be carried to the Potter's field, unwept and unloved? If so, no wonder Job cursed the day of his birth, and so many daily by poison, knife and fatal plunge 'jump the life to come.' "

But is this all?   To

> "Bear the whips and scorns of time,
> The oppressor's wrong, the proud man's contumely,
> The pangs of despis'd love, the law's delay,
> The insolence of office, and the spurns
> That patient merit of the unworthy takes?"

No, no! Turn to this dear old Book. Read its precious pages. Man was not made to suffer, and to die. He was made to be eternal, and to be eternally happy; and in his happiness to glorify God. This book declares that sin brought suffering and death into this world; and that all the sorrow and pain we see to-day is caused by sin. It was to save us from the guilt and power of sin that "God gave His only begotten Son, that whosoever believeth in Him should not perish, but have everlasting life." It teaches us it is the will of our Creator that all men should be saved. This life is only the beginning of life. What we call death is only an open door that opens into eternity; and this whole life is given us as a preparatory school for that eternal life beyond. In that eternal world are two abodes. One is the place of eternal punishment. It was not made for man, but for the devil and his angels. God warns us to shun that place of woe. By most solemn appeals and by picturing its horrors in most terrible imagery, He warns the sons of men to shun that death that never dies; and tells us plainly that only those who wilfully choose to serve Satan in this life shall finally be made to dwell with Satan.

The lost, however, fail of their true destiny. Man was ordained to life. His love for life is divine; and "all a man hath will he give for his life." So all who learn the lessons of life assigned them by God while in this preparatory school are promised glorious promotion. The lessons may be difficult sometimes. Sometimes they are "great tribulation," sometimes deepest sorrows, sometimes most painful afflictions; yet to all who learn the lessons of life, death is but a door opening into an eternal city whose streets are gold, whose walls are jasper, whose gates are pearl, whose inhabitants are never weary, nor sick, nor sad, whose streets and palaces are lighted by the countenance of the Lamb of God, whose king is the God of Glory. This city of eternal life is designed for all men, and all men may have it for their eternal home by simply choosing God as their master here, and living in accordance with His will.

The Bible represents man as a pilgrim, with staff in hand, toiling slowly along a foot path on a steep mountain side. Above him towers the massive granite peak, pile on pile, until lost in the clouds of heaven. Below him are crags, and precipice, and forests of pine and oak, until the far-a-way base is hidden by the gray mists of the valley. The pilgrim reaches a point where the path divides—one leading by gentle windings down the mountain; the other, straight and narrow, leading upward. He halts, hesitating which to take. Now he hears voices, whispering in his ear: "Come, go with us. Our home is at the foot of the mountain, and you will not have to climb that horrid hill. Our path is easy to travel—it slopes downward all the time. You can do as you please in this path, and not get out of it; for it is very broad. We have wine and refreshments at every turn of the path.

Come go with us. This is the popular way. The whole world goes this way." But the pilgrim hears voices in his other ear: "Come go with us. It is true the path is narrow; but it is so plain that 'a way-faring man, though a fool, need not' lose his way. It leads up hill, it is true; but we will help you climb it; and our king, who lives at the summit, always gives strength to the weak when they are climbing. Then too, at every step new beauties will unfold. Every ridge, as you ascend, will furnish you a more extended view. When we pass through the cloud we will find the land of Beulah where the sun is always shining; and when we reach the city at the summit our King himself will come out to welcome you, together with a host of saints and angels. They will welcome you with songs and shouts, and escort you to a mansion that is already prepared for you there. Come, come with us."

Here is the choice that settles our eternal destiny. The voices of God, and Duty, and truest Happiness exhorting the Pilgrim to eternity to climb; and the voices of Satan, and his servants, and appetites persuading him to take the popular path, because it leads down hill. Oh, young man! which path are you treading?

This, then, is the outline of what the Bible teaches: the divine origin of man, his true present condition, his true future destiny. This is the teaching, young men of the Association, you are to bring before your fellow-students day by day. In order to teach this, live it. But do not assume any sanctimonious airs. Don't whine. Don't talk through your nose. You will never win a College boy that way. They hate cant; but they appreciate genuine piety, and will respect the true, manly, Christian student.

"But they will not believe. College boys want something more real before they will believe." More real? Can anything be more real than spiritual phenomena? The teachings of the Bible are much more easy for me to believe than the teachings of science. In fact, I can conceive of no greater test of credulity than to believe the teachings of our present systems of science. Don't talk to me about spiritual things being hard to believe. A man that can believe in modern science can believe in anything.

. Take chemistry. The whole science of chemistry is based upon the atomic theory. What is that theory? That all existing matter is made up of less than seventy elementary substances; and that these elementary substances are made up of individual particles so small that they can not be divided, called atoms. This atom no man has ever seen, even with the most powerful microscope. No man has ever weighed it, although balances are made so delicate that you can weigh a black hair and a gray one from the same head, and the gray one will kick the beam. Not only has it never been seen nor weighed; but I, for one, can not conceive of a particle so small that it can not be made less. I can not conceive that a whole atom, and a half atom, and a millionth part of an atom are all the same size. But the chemist says I *must believe* it, whether I can *conceive* it or not. And this imaginary something called an atom, which has never been seen and can not be weighed, the chemist assumes he knows its size and also its weight; and wants me to believe that he can tell just how many of these atoms will unite with another set of atoms of a different substance, to form a new compound. Then on what basis does our whole science of chemistry rest? Upon the hypothesis, and only an hypothesis, that there are atoms; and although we can not see, weigh, nor conceive of an atom, yet that we know their size and weight. A man that can believe that can believe anything.

Turn to physics, and we have to use an equal amount of credulity. You hear the Professor lecturing most learnedly about light. He can tell you a thousand things about it: its wonderful freaks, its seven primary colors, the heat and actinic rays, its laws of refraction and reflection, its speed of 200,000 miles a second. You might imagine he knew all about light; but ask him a question or two. What is light? He will probably tell you, it is the vibration of a luminiferous ether that pervades all space. Then ask him, What is this ether, and what makes it vibrate? Ah, you have settled him now. No scientist ever saw an atom of this ether. He does not even know that such a thing exists. Yet, without knowing there is such a thing as ether, he goes on to tell you that there is ether, that it vibrates, that he can measure a vibration to the ten-millionth part of an inch, and that 758,840,000,000,000 of these vibrations strike my eye every second. Does the Bible ask a man to believe anything more utterly unreasonable than that?

It is the same with heat, magnetism, electricity, and gravitation. No man has ever seen these things, or knows what they are, or whether they are anything at all. The whole of our scientific systems is built upon hypotheses or assumptions. We have the phenomena; and with all of their apparent extravagances and absurdities our sciences are the best explanations we can give to account for the phenomena. So we believe in them.

But while we are so ready to believe in scientific hypotheses, why are some so ready to doubt the truths of the Bible?

Talk as we may, there are spiritual phenomena in this world just as real as the material phenomena. The testimony is clear. Why not believe the man when he testifies to spiritual phenomena as when he testifies to material phenomena?

I read in a book that by putting a piece of zinc in diluted sulphuric acid a gas will be given off, called hydrogen. Certain tests are given. I am induced to try the experiment. I get my acid, dilute it as directed, and put in my zinc. At once the liquid begins to bubble. I do not see anything; but as directed I hold my wide-mouthed bottle over the escape tube a little while. I see nothing in the bottle—I feel nothing in it. It is just as it was before to all appearances; but on applying a match to the bottle an explosion occurs. Then I must acknowledge that one test given by the book is true. I now catch the gas in a different shaped vessel, and on applying the match, find it burns with a pale blue flame and intense heat. So I run through every test named in the book, and prove them every one. I do not now hesitate to say the book is true. I tell my friends about it. They test it and find it true also. No one now doubts the statement of the author. The tests have been verified, and can be verified by any one who desires to prove them.

I read in another book of certain symptoms of mind and body which denote a fatal disease. I find I have all

4

the symptoms described. The book goes on to prescribe a certain course of treatment by which one so diseased may be cured. I hasten at once to use the remedies. It works like a charm, and soon I am well. In my joy at my recovery I go tell my friend all about it, both the disease and the cure. He says, "Why, I, too, am afflicted that same way. You say it cured you?" "Yes." "Then I'll try it too." He does, and is cured. So are a score of others to whom we tell the story. It is now found that this disease is universal. In fact, the book said it was. What a demand now springs up for the book that tells of a cure *that does cure!* How valuable, even above price, is now the book of healing!

Now, in these material things men do not doubt; or if they doubt, they still lay aside doubts sufficiently to test the thing. Why then should they doubt in spiritual things, absolutely refusing to test them. I read in this book (the Bible) that certain spiritual phenomena will take place under certain stated conditions. I try it, and find it true. I bear testimony to this fact, and ask you to try the experiment for yourselves. You believed me when I told you of the hydrogen experiment, and proved it for yourselves. Why not believe me in this spiritual case?

I read in this book that there is a terrible disease among men called sin. I find I have all the symptoms described. They are all plainly developed in my case. The book that describes the disease tells me that the disease brings death, eternal death, unless cured; and I tremble with terror. I read on, and find that a great Physician has prescribed a sure cure for all cases, without money, and

without price. I go at once to Him, use the remedies He
prescribes, and soon find I am healed, just as He said I
would be. The cure is wrought; and I know it. He
said that I should be a new creature. I feel that I am.
He said that the things I once loved I would hate. It
is even so. He said the things that I once hated I would
love. I find it is true. He said that hate, envy, malice,
and revenge would be taken from me, and I would love
everybody. I find it true. He said that a great peace
would spring up in my soul, like a well of water, or as a
smooth-flowing river. It is true. I fully realize the fact
that the disease is gone, and my health is recovered. In
my joy I tell my friend. He tries it, and finds a like result. We two tell others. Every one that tries it finds
it to be true in every particular. The good news spreads
from land to land, from nation to nation, until tens of
millions of all peoples, of all nations, of all kindreds and
tongues, rise up and say "It is true. Every word is true.
I have proved it for myself. Glory to God in the highest
for this great salvation."

This is no stretch of imagination; it is the true history
of this God-given book for the past nineteen hundred
years. No one who has honestly tried it has ever found
it false in a single particular. Then why do some hold
aloof and say, "I doubt the truth of that book?" It is
because they have never thoroughly tested it. Many of
those who doubt do so through ignorance. It is your
part, brethren of the Young Men's Christian Association
to use every effort to dispel such ignorance and consequent
doubt from among your associates in the College.

Go forward then to hold up the Bible standard of holiness and salvation. Let your associates see that true religion is a practical factor in daily life. Do all that you can, by word and example, to sow the good seed of eternal life; and when the harvest of the world shall come, and the angelic reapers shall go forth, may God grant that you may appear before the Lord of the harvest bearing precious sheaves, as the result of your piety and fidelity during the excitements and difficulties of the days spent in the halls of St. John's. Amen!

Alumni Day.

The morning of WEDNESDAY the 26th of June—ALUMNI DAY—dawned very inauspiciously for a celebration in the open air. But to the great relief of many anxious ones, before the hour appointed for the beginning of the ceremonies, the rain, which had fallen in torrents, ceased. Occasional light showers fell during the exercises, but caused no interruption. In accordance with the ceremony observed at the formal opening of the College in 1789, and in response to a published invitation, members of the Board of Visitors and Governors, members of the Faculty, *Doctor Fell in academic costume, and numerous Alumni, met at the State House about 10 o'clock, and under the escort of Students of the College, in military uniform, commanded by Lieut. Mitchell F. Jamar, United States Army, a member of the Faculty, preceded by the United States Naval Academy Band, marched in procession by way of Maryland Avenue and Prince George Street to the College Campus, where under a large marquee, provided in anticipation of an assemblage exceeding the accommodation of McDowell Hall, and erected beneath the sheltering branches of the Old Poplar, a numerous audience had already gathered. A suitable platform, tastefully decorated with bunting and flags, had been

*The Honorary Degree of LL. D. had been conferred on Principal Fell a few days before by Hampden Sidney College, Virginia.

placed adjoining the Old Tree. Governor Jackson, with other members of the Board of Visitors and Governors, members of the Faculty, and others, occupied seats on the platform.

Mr. FRANK. H. STOCKETT of the Class of '41, as President of the Board of Visitors and Governors, presided. The exercises were opened with the following prayer by the Rev. ORLANDO HUTTON, D. D., of the Class of '34:

ALMIGHTY GOD, the Author of all being, and the fountain of all wisdom and knowledge; who hast formed our bodies and endued us with reasonable souls; regard with Thy favor and visit with Thy blessing this Institution established for the promotion of sound learning and Christian education.

Give Thy holy Light for illumination and guidance to Thy servants now and here assembled to engage in mutual counsels and united efforts for the advancement of the high and noble ends for which this College was founded. Animate us with a true zeal for Thy Glory and an earnest purpose to promote such wise measures as will conduce to the welfare of this College which has been to us an Alma Mater in all fostering care for intellectual culture and moral training.

We bless Thy Holy Name that under Thy Divine Providence this venerable Institution has been brought through all the vicissitudes of the past to celebrate this day, under happy auspices, the Centenary of its foundation. And we earnestly pray that like as in the past distinguished sons have gone forth from these walls to render honorable service to their country, so in the future may many other sons yet go forth to reflect by their eminent character and services like honor upon their Alma Mater.

Raise up, we pray Thee, friends and patrons to enable those charged with its governorship and its educational work to carry into effect its good designs. Inspire all who are officially connected with this Institution with a due sense of their solemn trusts, and

with wisdom and strength for their faithful fulfilment. And may
all who are privileged to enjoy the educational advantages here
provided, have the docility and the diligence for the successful pur-
suit of knowledge and the ready mind to follow the counsels of
Godly wisdom and experience.

Let Thy Protection guard, and Thy Blessing rest upon, all who
are gathered here in these commemoration festivities. May all
be endued with the spirit to seek and do the things that will advance
Thy Glory and the good of Thy people in our land. All which
we ask in the Name and for the Sake of JESUS CHRIST our
LORD—*Amen.*

A chorus of fifty voices, under the direction of Mr.
George H. Shafer, than sang to the air of *"God Save
the King,"* the Band accompanying, the following Ode,
written for the occasion by Mr. Nicholas Brewer of the
Class of '46.

Greeting to St. John's.

All hail! St. John's to thee!
Past is a century
  Thy natal day,
Since from yon State House tall,
The Sons of "KING WILLIAM'S" all
To Old McDowell Hall,
  Wended their way.*

There 'neath its pillar'd dome,
Dreamed in their student-home
  Sons of our Sires;

* For an account of this procession, see Record of Proceedings of the Visitors and
Governors of St. John's College.

There plodded side by side,
In sports and studies vied,
Worshipped in love and pride
    At thy altar fires.

All hail! Lov'd College Green!
Thy sward full oft hath been
    Bed of the brave.
France and the Father-Land *
Here meeting, hand in hand,
March'd forth, a gallant band,
    Our freedom to save.

All hail! Thou grand old tree,
Emblem of Liberty! †
    Of thee we sing.
Here 'neath thy ample shade,
Oft our forefathers strayed,
And we in boyhood played.
    To thee we'll cling.

All hail! Old College bell!
Thy silv'ry tones yet swell
    O'er Severn's shore.
Thy call we now obey,
On this centennial day,
And our glad homage pay,
    As in days of yore.

St. John's where'er we roam,
To thee lov'd College home,
    Fondly we turn.
Here friends of early years,
Comrades in hopes and fears,
Faithful in smiles and tears,
    Their incense burn.

* Reference is here had to La Fayette, Rochambeau, De Kalb, and Steuben.
† The Old Tulip Poplar Tree was once familiarly known as " The Liberty Tree."

Long may thy courts resound,
Thy halls with youth abound,
    As in days past!
Thy future plenty crown,
Honors thy sorrows drown,
Heav'n on thy foemen frown,
    And bless thee at last!

Immediately following this, there was sung with the same accompaniment, the National Anthem, written by FRANCIS SCOTT KEY, an Alumnus of the College of the Class of '96.

The Star Spangled Banner.

O SAY, can you see, by the dawn's early light,
    What so proudly we hailed, at the twilight's last gleaming?
Whose broad stripes and bright stars through the perilous fight,
    O'er the ramparts we watched, were so gallantly streaming;
And the rockets' red glare, the bombs bursting in air,
Gave proof through the night that our flag was still there:
    O say, does that Star Spangled Banner yet wave
    O'er the land of the free and the home of the brave?

On that shore, dimly seen through the mists of the deep,
    Where the foe's haughty host in dread silence reposes,
What is that which the breeze, o'er the towering steep,
    As it fitfully blows, now conceals, now discloses?
Now it catches the gleam of the morning's first beam,
In full glory reflected now shines in the stream:
    'Tis the Star Spangled Banner; O long may it wave
    O'er the land of the free and the home of the brave!

And where are the foes who so vauntingly swore
   That the havoc of war, and the battle's confusion,
A home and a country should leave us no more:
   Their blood has washed out their foul footsteps' pollution;
No refuge could save the hireling and slave
From the terror of flight, or the gloom of the grave;
   And the Star Spangled Banner in triumph doth wave
   O'er the land of the free and the home of the brave!

O thus be it ever, when freemen shall stand
   Between their loved homes and the war's desolation;
Blest with victory and peace, may the heav'n-rescued land
   Praise the Power that hath made and preserved us a nation!
Then conquer we must, when our cause it is just,
And this be our motto, "In God is our trust;"
   And the Star Spangled Banner in triumph shall wave
   O'er the land of the free and the home of the brave!

Mr. FRANK. H. STOCKETT, then addressed the assemblage as follows:

GENTLEMEN OF THE BOARD OF VISITORS AND GOVERNORS OF ST. JOHN'S COLLEGE: GENTLEMEN OF THE FACULTY: LADIES AND GENTLEMEN:

By some misapprehension, or oversight, it has been published that an address was to be delivered by me to-day before this audience.

There was no such understanding on my part. At no time did I ever so agree; and as mutuality is essential to the validity of a contract, I shall not hesitate to avail myself of this plea to save you from any such infliction.

If, therefore, you have by reason of such announcement, been beguiled into the expectation of any such treat, you are destined to go away disappointed.

Such a loss, will I am sure, be more than compensated by the intellectual feast to be supplied by those who are to be introduced to you by me.

My duties are much simpler, better adapted to my acquirements, and more considerate to you.

They are merely to announce the occasion of your being here to-day, and to present to you those who are to furnish the feast. The occasion of our meeting is one of unusual significance.

It is to honor the CENTENARY of old St. John's; to manifest our veneration and love for an Institution that has done so much good for the State, and has been of such incalculable benefit to the City of Annapolis in particular.

To this celebration we extend to you a most sincere and cordial welcome.

Mr. STOCKETT, at the close of his address of welcome, presented Mr. PHILIP RANDALL VOORHEES, of New York, of the class of '55.

LADIES AND GENTLEMEN, BROTHERS ALUMNI, AND STUDENTS OF SAINT JOHN'S,—When the Committee, appointed to arrange a programme of commemorative ceremonies appropriate to the Centenary of St. John's College, requested me, through Principal Fell, to prepare and deliver before you, as part of said programme for Alumni Day, a historical sketch of the College I felt at first no ordinary embarrassment. Nevertheless, impelled by a sense of duty, I promptly accepted the honor conferred. But, though painfully conscious then of my lack of literary qualifications, as my mind dwelt more upon the subject and the occasion, and as I refreshed my recollections of St. John's antecedents by the perusal of the authorities at my command, my first embarrassment was increased tenfold. I can, therefore, only pray you to bear patiently the detention which I shall impose upon you, by covering with the mantle of your charity my temerity in appearing before you in any other capacity than that of a hearer and learner. Were it not that the task assigned me is to do but little more than chronicle in one paper, in as orderly sequence as I may, events which have been more or less separately or segregatively reviewed before you at different times, I could not have consented to stand here in the footsteps of those Alumni, and others distinguished in letters, who have in such numbers heretofore addressed audiences such as this, nor to break silence by any words of mine, while mindful of the stirring eloquence of those who have so often urged upon the people of the State, and their representatives in General Assembly, the merits of this venerable institution of learning and its claims to their fostering care. But it is eminently proper that a review of St. John's history should be read before its sons and others in celebration of the One Hundredth Anniversary of its natal collegiate day, or, more correctly speaking perhaps, its baptismal day, albeit such history is so well known by its alumni present. My only regret is, therefore, that some one more competent to do the full measure of justice to the subject should not have been selected for the historic work of the day.

Bolingbroke says in his letters on the Study and Uses of History—attributing the remark to Dionysius of Halicarnassus—that "history is philosophy teaching by ex-

amples." If this be so, then indeed Brothers Alumni
the history of our Alma Mater, from her earliest past,
is part and parcel of a grand philosophy, teaching all the
virtues that go to make the patriot, the statesman, and
the man, and we may not too warmly nor too jealously
cherish the deeds and memories of her distinguished sons,
as well as the times *quorum magna pars fuerunt.* It is
needless to remind this audience that the names of many
of St. John's sons are enrolled not alone in the annals of
the State, but in those of the Nation as well. They
have given their Alma Mater a historic place in the
temple of fame as enduring as the temple itself. As an
alumnus bearing the revered name of Pinkney so felicit-
ously said on Commencement Day in 1855, when coup-
ling the name of Key with the College,—"She has given
the Star Spangled Banner to the nation, and made other
offerings of which it is not necessary for me to speak."
A College necrology has also, fortunately, been preserved,
which perpetuates, in the archives of the Alumni, the
memory of the virtues of deceased brethren. This necrology, first suggested, and its preparation personally begun,
by a former Principal, Dr. Humphreys, has been extended
and continued, you need not be reminded how faithfully,
by the facile pen of Mr. John G. Proud, of the Class of '34,
whose name, alas, now adorns that roll of the dead, upon
which his labors of love and painstaking research had
stamped the seal of truth. May the Alumni ever cherish
the memory of this brother, who by tongue and pen,
both in forcible prose and graceful verse, has expressed
so much devotion to St. John's and her sons.

Though St. John's first opened its doors on the 11th
day of November, 1789, under the name it now bears,

the history of the attempts which finally eventuated in its establishment begins at a much earlier date.

A brief sketch here of the origin of the city where St. John's is located may not be out of place, before proceeding to the history of the College itself.

When, in the Province of Maryland, under the Proprietary Government of Cecilius Calvert, the second Lord Baltimore, a colony had already become settled at St. Mary's, then the capital of the Province, though the red Indian still hunted on the shores of the Severn, and the "Old Poplar Tree of the Old College Green" under which we are now assembled, then stood the pride of the "forest primeval," a small band of Puritans, in 1649, driven by the rigid execution against them of the laws then existing in the Province of Virginia, "removed themselves," their "families and estates into the Province of Maryland, being thereto invited by Capt. William Stone, then Governor for Lord Baltimore, with the promise of liberty in religion and privileges of English subjects." Captain Stone's appointment as Governor, it is said, depended upon his bringing five hundred immigrants into the Province, hence his invitation to these Puritans. This company of about one hundred immigrants first settled on Greenberry's Point, then known as Town Neck, which with the opposite point, now known as Horn's Point, or Horn Point, forms the entrance or mouth of the Severn River. But, only eight individuals patenting the Neck, which consisted of two hundred and fifty acres, the settlement spread over more territory and occupied both banks of the Severn, the entire settlement being named "Providence." In 1650 this settlement sent two burgesses to the General Assembly at St. Mary's, one of the two being elected speaker of the lower House. This Assembly passed an Act erecting Providence into a county, giving it the name of "Anne Arundel"—the maiden name of Lady Baltimore.

The Puritan settlers having taken a modified oath—relinquishing no rights as English subjects—professedly acquiesced in Lord Baltimore's Proprietary Government under Governor Stone, thereby securing only warrants of survey, not land patents, except in a few instances, to secure which patents would have required the oath of allegiance to the Lord Proprietor. In July of 1650 Governor Stone visited the settlers, and commissioned Mr. Edward Lloyd to be Commander of Anne Arundel County.

This Mr. Lloyd, though he returned to England, where he died in London in 1695, left a son in the Province, in possession of an estate on the Eastern shore. This son is the ancestor of the Lloyd family whose representatives, in successive generations, have given distinguished service to the State, notably in its councils and thrice in its gubernatorial chair. In 1651, Mr. Lloyd, empowered by the Governor, granted a warrant to Thomas Todd for land covering the greater part of what is now Annapolis, Lord Baltimore's rent-roll, showing that on the 8th of July, 1651, one hundred acres were surveyed for said Todd. In the following November a parcel of one hundred acres, in the possession of Philip Hammond, was surveyed for Richard Acton, and called "Acton." This land, from its name, will be recognized by many in my audience as forming part of Annapolis.

But before the Puritans were firmly here settled, stirring events happened between 1653 and 1657. In 1654,

Cromwell was proclaimed in the province by Governor Stone, who resigned his office, submitting his authority to the Government of the Protector. But, upbraided by Lord Baltimore, he engaged in the "battle of the Severn," on Sunday, March, 25, 1655, leading Lord Baltimore's forces from St. Mary's against the Puritans of the Severn under Captain Fuller, in which battle the latter were victorious, losing but six killed, while Governor Stone's forces had twenty killed and thirty wounded, the Governor himself being among the latter. The scene of the battle, supposed to have been on Horn Point, was long called the "Papists' Pound," and the "men of Severn" governed themselves thereafter until 1657, when settlement was effected, through intermediaries and Lord Baltimore, in England. During these difficulties in 1654, the name of Anne Arundel County had been dropped, the Puritans again calling it Providence, but in 1657, by an order of Council, Providence County was re-named "Anne Arundel," the "men of Severn" having virtually ruled the whole province for nearly eight years.

Of this "war," the Rev. Ethan Allen in his "Historical Notices of St. Ann's Parish in Anne Arundel County," published in 1857, from which the facts herein recited, bearing upon the origin of Annapolis, are mainly gleaned, remarks: "If, as alleged, the Lord Protector had confirmed the reducement of Maryland from under Lord Baltimore by the Commissioners, then this was a war against him ; and the St. Mary's government was a rebellion against the government established. If, however, the St. Marians could conquer, their right to govern would be as good at least as was Cromwell's by which he held the government of England."

In 1662, "Todd's Range" was surveyed, on the south side of the Severn, and on the 16th of September, 1670, "Todd's Harbor," was surveyed. This is said to be the site of Annapolis, which, in 1683, under the name of the "Town at Proctor's," was made a Port of Entry.

In 1689 Proprietary Government ceased in Maryland, and the Colonial Governor, Sir Lyonel Copley, assumed office April 9, 1692. Dying the next year, he was succeeded by Governor Francis Nicholson, and a General Assembly met at St. Mary's on the 21st of September, 1694. This Assembly passed an Act making the "town land at Severn in Anne Arundel County, where the town was formerly" (doubtless the place called in 1683 the Town at Proctor's) a town port and place of trade under the name of "Anne Arundel Town," and "Major Hammond, Major Edward Dorsey, Mr. John Bennett, Mr. John Dorsey, Mr. Andrew Norwood, Mr. Philip Howard, Mr. James Saunders and the Hon. Nicholas Greenberry, Esq., a member of the Council, were appointed to purchase and lay out one hundred acres of land in lots and streets, and with open places to be left on which to erect a church, market-house, and other public buildings." The same Assembly passed an Act for the erection of a Court House, and the seat of government was permanently removed from St. Mary's to Anne Arundel Town, whose name was changed to Annapolis, in honor of Queen Anne as is recited in its charter subsequently received. The Court House, also used as a State House, was completed in 1697, but destroyed by fire in 1704. Another building was erected on its site, but torn down in 1769 to give place to the present edifice, supposed to have been designed by a pupil of Sir Christopher Wren, the corner stone of which was laid in 1772 by Governor Eden, the last of the Colonial Governors. Historic Annapolis received its charter in 1708 from the Hon. John Seymour, Colonial Governor, and thus became a city with due corporate powers and privileges.

Prior, however, to the removal of the seat of Government from St. Mary's, the *first* effort was made, by the Legislature in 1671, to establish a college in the province of Maryland, from which, slowly, through many further attempts, St. John's was evolved. But the two Houses of the Legislature disagreed upon certain amendments• passed by the upper House, and the bill failed to be enacted. Next, in 1694, Governor Nicholson, the new Governor, proposed in a message to the Legislature "that a way be found for the building of a Free School for the Province," and offered to give money for its maintenance. The Governor's proposition was approved by the General Assembly, which offered subscriptions of tobacco, and suggested that two Free Schools be established, one at Oxford on the Eastern shore of the State, and the other at Severn on the Western shore.* The Rev. Ethan Allen, in his Notes before mentioned, thus refers to these offers: "The Governor proposed to give £50 for the building of the school house and £25 per annum to the master. Sir Thomas Lawrence, Secretary, gave 5000 lbs. towards the building, and 2000 lbs. tobacco per annum to the master. The House contributed 45,000 lbs. tobacco towards the

*These facts as to early efforts to found a College in Maryland are recited in a brief historical sketch attached to a printed catalogue of St. John's, published in 1874, referring to a paper in the Educational Bureau in Washington.

building; and of the members of the Council, Cols.
Jowles, Robotham, Greenberry and Brooks, 2000 lbs.
each; Hutchinson and Frisby 1000 lbs. each, Thomas
Brooke, Esq., £5 sterling towards the master's support
and Edmund Randolph £10 sterling." No practical
measures, however, immediately flowed from these proceedings. But soon after, in 1696, under the reign of
William the Third, the Colonial Legislature passed a
"Petitionary Act" praying that Sovereign for the establishment of a Free School or schools in Anne Arundel
Town upon the Severn River, with corporate powers and
privileges, and for the establishment of a similar Free
School in every county of the Province. The latter part
of this proposed measure seems, however, not to have
been prosecuted further until 1723, when an Act was
passed for the erection of "one school in each county, as
near the centre thereof as might be and as should be most
convenient for the boarding of children." The petitionary Act, above mentioned, also prayed that the school or
schools to be established thereunder in Anne Arundel
Town should be devoted to the education of the youth of
the Province in good letters and manners, including
Latin, Greek and writing, under the Royal patronage,
with the Archbishop of Canterbury as the Chancellor;
and that, to perpetuate the memory of the Sovereign, the
first school there established should be called King William's School; to be managed by trustees, to be appointed
by the King, and by others, named in the Act, among the
names mentioned being found those of the Governor,
Francis Nicholson, Esq.; the Hon. Sir Thomas Lawrence,
Bart.; Col. George Robotham; Col. John Addison, of the

Provincial Council, and the Rev. Peregrine Coney.
Though this petitionary Act was not declared in force
until the time of Queen Anne in 1704, yet its "Rectors,
Visitors and Governors," apparently in anticipation of
the royal approval, opened "King William's School" at
Annapolis, then but recently known as Anne Arundel
Town, either in 1701 or 1704—the exact date does not
appear certain. Governor Nicholson gave to the school
a lot, with a house thereon, and the Legislature appropriated money to build the school house, which was completed about the time of, or shortly before, the opening
of the school. The school house, built of brick and stone,
was located on the south side of the State House, within
the present limits of its grounds, about where the De
Kalb monument now stands, and about opposite the
Eastern end of the street still called School street.

From this beginning, at the dawn of the eighteenth
century, King William's School appears to have flourished
for about eighty-five years, passing successfully through
the perturbations of the Revolutionary War, and edu-
cating for the State and Nation sons distinguished in
the early history of the country. Among its pupils William Pinkney, whose fame, too broad to be appropriated
by any one State, is a heritage unto the Nation. This
school, as we shall shortly see, was finally merged in St.
John's College, delivering over to it its head master, as
a professor, and students, funds and other property.

In the meantime, in 1732, as appears by the historical
sketch above mentioned, "Proposals for founding a College at Annapolis" were read in the upper House of Assembly and recommended to the consideration of the

lower House, but no legislative effect was given to these proposals. In 1763 this project was revived. A committee presented a report recommending "that the house in the city of Annapolis which was intended for the Governor of this Province, be completely finished and used for the College proposed to be established." The measure was passed by the lower House, providing for the necessary expenses and annual pay of the Faculty, to consist of seven masters, to be provided with five servants, but it failed to pass the upper House. But the intent to establish a College at Annapolis seemed still to linger in the popular mind; for, in a letter dated Oct. 4, 1773, William Eddis, the Surveyor of Customs at the port of Annapolis, writes, to a friend in England, that the Legislature of the province had determined "to endow and form a College for the education of youth in every liberal and useful branch of science" which, "as it will be conducted under excellent regulations, will shortly preclude the necessity of crossing the Atlantic for the completion of a classical and polite education." He also states that it had been determined to repair the damages to the "melancholy and mouldering monument" formerly designed for the Governor's mansion, and to devote it "to the purposes of collegiate education, for which every circumstance contributes to render it truly eligible." As we shall presently see, this "melancholy and mouldering monument," to use his own expression, was finally selected and devoted to the purposes of a "classical and polite education." But the Revolutionary War soon followed this stormy period of the country's history, during which period, the patriotic citizens of Annapolis caused the owner or consignees of a tea-ship, the brig "Peggy Stewart," themselves to apply the torch and burn the ship as well as the cargo. The hopes and efforts of those who sought to give to the State the educational advantage of a college or university were thus doomed to further disappointment and delay, so that not until 1782 did the Legislature of the State, the Colonial Government having been dethroned, again consider the matter. But when scarcely out of the throes of the Revolution, and before the definitive treaty of peace of 1784 had been concluded, it was proposed to establish two colleges on the shores of the Chesapeake Bay, with a view to their subsequent union under "one supreme legislative and visitorial jurisdiction, as distinct branches or members of the same State University," (Charter of Washington College, Act of April, 1782, Chap. 8.) In pursuance of this policy Washington College was founded in 1782 on the Eastern, and, two years later, St. John's College on the Western shore. These facts, with the exception of the tea-burning incident, are gathered from the historical sketch and the laws above mentioned.

By Chapter 37 of the Laws of 1784, the Legislature of the new and Sovereign State of Maryland, *in consideration* of the contributions voluntarily made and to be made by individual or corporate subscribers, for the purpose of founding St. John's College, granted to its original corporators, "The Visitors and Governors," to be thereafter elected by such subscribers, a charter, by the XIXth section of which the sum of one thousand seven hundred and fifty pounds current money was annually and *forever* granted as a donation by the public to the use of said

College, to be applied by the Visitors and Governors to the payment of salaries to the Principal, Professors and Tutors of the said College.

But, on the 25th of January, 1805, the Legislature passed an Act (Chap. 85) repealing the XIXth section of the charter and the annual appropriation, therein provided for, was withheld from the College. The Act of repeal, however, was passed by but a small majority. It would be unprofitable to seek or to discuss here the reasons that prompted this action on the part of the people's representatives. The action itself has been fitly characterized, in no measured terms, time and again by eloquent tongues, and it will be sufficient to remark here that, while in the sixteenth year of its active usefulness, and when promising increased advantages for the future, this action so crippled the institution that it did not, for years as a college, recover from the blow, if indeed its whole developement thereafter was not, for all time, modified. But in 1811 the State voted an annual donation of one thousand dollars, and in 1821 authorized the College to raise, by a lottery, a sum not exceeding eighty thousand dollars, of which amount the sum of twenty thousand dollars was realized, and invested as a college fund. In 1832, by joint resolution, No. 41, two thousand dollars was added by the State to the annual sum of one thousand dollars theretofore voted, conditioned upon the Visitors and Governors agreeing to accept the same in full satisfaction of all claims against the State for the unpaid sums provided for in the charter. Despairing of better terms, and the money being greatly needed, the Visitors and Governors, under such circumstances of practical, if not legal, duress, acceded to and executed a release. Subsequently, by Resolution No. 4 of 1858, the Legislature authorized a suit to be brought to test the constitutionality of the repeal of the XIXth section of the charter. Such a suit was accordingly brought, in Equity, the Governor appearing for the State as a defendant. The bill charged that the State by such repeal had violated the provisions of a solemn contract. The Court of Appeals, on a case stated from the Court below, so held (15 Md. Reports, 330). But the same Court also held later, when payment was sought to be obtained by proceedings for a mandamus to the accounting officers of the Treasury, that the Visitors and Governors "having accepted the proposals of the Legislature and by their solemn and formal release having discharged and extinguished the claim made here, have deprived themselves of the power as well as right to assert and again maintain it." The Court, having reached this conclusion, expressed no opinion upon the point raised by the defense, that a mandamus, under the facts of the case, was not the proper remedy. (23 Md. Rep., 629).

The legal proceedings rested here, although an appeal from this decision to the Supreme Court of the United States was advised by eminent authority, upon the ground that the Visitors and Governors had exceeded the authority conferred upon them, in executing such release, the case being one in which the act complained of involved the question of a violation of the constitution of the United States, Section X of Article I of which declares that "No State shall pass any Law impairing the Obligation of Contracts."

But in 1866, the Visitors and Governors, ever faithful to the interests of the College, memorialized the Legislature, urging, in the strongest terms, the hardship of the situation and their dislike to appeal to a jurisdiction outside of the State in search of any relief which it was competent for the State itself by legislative action to grant. Whereupon the Legislature, mindful of the situation, voted to restore the amount of unpaid annuities which had, through fortuitous circumstances, accrued within the preceding five years—the war period—during which the College was closed. An additional appropriation of twelve thousand dollars was also voted, to be paid annually, on and after June 1st, 1868, for the next five years. (Act of 1866, Chap. 101).

Of the Acts of 1872, Section 1 of Chapter 393, appropriated, in addition "to the sum of three thousand dollars now annually paid," the sum of twelve thousand dollars annually on and after the first day of June, 1873, for and during the term of six years. Section 2 granted ten thousand dollars per annum for the board, fuel, lights and washing of two students from each senatorial district to be given free tuition by the College. Section 3 gave in gross the sum of five thousand dollars for increasing and improving the college library, laboratory, philosophical apparatus and cabinet.

Of the Acts of 1878, Section 1 of Chapter 315, in addition to the permanent annuity of three thousand dollars, continued the appropriation of 1872, of twelve thousand dollars, then about to expire, for and during the term of two years on and after the first day of October, 1878. Section 2 repealed section 2 of Chapter 393 of the Acts of 1872, and granted instead two hundred dollars per annum, beginning the first day of October, 1878, for every student provided for in said repealed section, until the number of said students should be reduced to *one* for each senatorial district, when, and thereafter, it granted the sum of five thousand two hundred dollars per annum for the board, fuel, lights and washing of such total number of students, to be given free tuition by the college—under the conditions of good character, pecuniary inability, and other qualifications imposed. The statute-book, to the present, shows no further financial legislation in aid of the college, except the sums of seven thousand five hundred dollars appropriated by the Act of 1882, chapter 459; and four thousand dollars by the Act of 1886, chapter 402; and two thousand two hundred and fifty-six dollars, amount of two years interest on the indebtedness of the College, appropriated by the Act of 1888, Chapter 408.

This cursory sketch of the financial relations which have existed between the parent State and St. John's from its birth, while showing a certain liberality, also shows to what slight approach towards the real necessities of the case such assistance could only go. Such digression from the orderly narration of events in the history of the College has been made, however, solely with a view of avoiding the interruption of such narration by the introduction, at intervals, of financial details which it seemed better to connect and mass in one statement.

Returning now to the year 1784—the date when, as we have seen, the legal existence of St. John's, *eo nomine*, began—we find many of Maryland's sons, distinguished in both the State and Nation, among the promoters in the

endeavor to found a great college of that name. Active
among these promoters were Samuel Chase, William Paca,
Thomas Stone, Charles Carroll of Carrollton, famous as
signers of the Declaration of Independence, Daniel of St.
Thomas Jenifer, John Eagar Howard, Richard Ridgely,
George Plater, Luther Martin, Jeremiah Townley Chase,
Alexander Contee Hanson, the Right Reverend Thomas
John Claggett, Robert Bowie, the Eversfields, Benedict
Calvert, Benjamin Stoddard, George Diggs, Gerard B.
Causin, John Chapman, John Sterett, Daniel McMachen,
Daniel Bowly, Robert Gilmor, Otho H. Williams, George
Lux, and others of like excellence and influence.

Under these auspicious influences St. John's received
its charter from the State of Maryland. The act of incor-
poration, constituting this charter, (Chapter 37 of the
Acts of 1784, consisting of the preamble and thirty-six
sections) is entitled:

"An Act for founding a College on the western shore
of this State and constituting the same, together with
Washington College on the eastern shore, into one university, by the name of The University of Maryland."

This charter in its preamble declares: "Whereas institutions for the liberal education of youth in the principles of virtue, knowledge and useful literature, are of
the highest benefit to society, in order to train up and
perpetuate a succession of able and honest men for dis-
charging the various offices and duties of life, both civil
and religious, with usefulness and reputation, and such
institutions of learning have accordingly been promoted
and encouraged by the wisest and best regulated States:
And whereas it appears to this general assembly that

many public spirited individuals, from an earnest desire to promote the founding a college or seminary of learning on the western shore of this State, have subscribed and procured subscriptions to a considerable amount, and there is reason to believe that very large additions will be obtained to the same throughout the different counties of the said shore, if they were made capable in law to receive and apply the same towards founding and carrying on a college or general seminary of learning, with such statutory plan, and with such legislative assistance and direction, as the general assembly might think fit; and this general assembly highly approving those generous exertions of individuals, are desirous to embrace the present favorable occasion of peace and prosperity for making lasting provision for the encouragement and advancement of all useful knowledge and literature through every part of this State."

By the second section immediately following the preamble, it is in part enacted: "That a college or general seminary of learning, by the name of Saint John's, be established on the said western shore, upon the following fundamental and inviolable principles, namely; first, the said college shall be founded and maintained for ever, upon a most liberal plan, for the benefit of youth of every religious denomination, who shall be freely admitted to equal privileges and advantages of education, and to all the literary honors of the college, according to their merit, without requiring or enforcing any religious or civil test, or urging their attendance upon any particular religious worship or service, other than what they have been educated in, or have the consent and approbation of their parents

or guardians to attend; nor shall any preference be given
in the choice of a principal, vice-principal, or other professor, master or tutor, in the said college, on account
of his particular religious profession, having regard solely
to his moral character and literary abilities, and other
necessary qualifications to fill the place for which he shall
be chosen."

By the third section, The Right Reverend John Carroll
(the first Catholic Archbishop of America) and the Reverend Doctors William Smith and Patrick Allison (eminent divines respectively of the Protestant Episcopal and
Presbyterian Churches), Richard Spring, John Steret,
George Diggs, Esquires, "and such other persons as they
or any two of them may appoint," were "authorized to
solicit and receive subscriptions and contributions for the
said intended college and seminary of universal learning."

It is needless to add that we are told that these eminent
men, of all shades of faith, cordially assisted and harmo-
niously engaged in the good work of securing funds for,
and of assisting in, the founding of the intended seminary
of universal learning, "upon a most liberal plan for the
benefit of youth, of every religious denomination," which
should require no religious test, nor "attendance upon
any particular religious worship or service."

By the same third section it is provided that each subscriber, or class of subscribers, of one thousand dollars
shall be entitled to elect "one Visitor or Governor" of
the College.

By the fourth section it is enacted that when the Visitors and Governors were so elected, they should meet and
take upon themselves their trust and should then be "one

community, corporation and body politic, to have continuance forever by the name of the Visitors and Governors of St. John's College in the State of Maryland; and by the same name shall have perpetual succession."

The seventh section, in case Annapolis should be selected by the Visitors and Governors as the place for establishing the College, grants them a lot of four acres of ground in fee, whereon St. John's should be located. This lot contained the monumental ruin, mentioned in Mr. Eddis' letter, in 1773, which will be described further on.

By the thirty-third section it is enacted that Washington College and St. John's College "shall be and they are hereby declared to be one University, by the name of the University of Maryland, whereof the Governor of the State for the time being shall be chancellor, and the principal of one of said colleges shall be vice-chancellor, either by seniority or election, according to such rule or by-law of the University as may afterwards be made in that case." This legalized union never reaching consummation, St. John's took its departure from King William's School, alone, for weal or woe, among the educational institutions of the young Republic.

The preamble to the consolidation Act of 1785, chapter 39, informs us that, "The Rector, Governors, Trustees and Visitors of King William's School, in the city of Annapolis, have represented to the general assembly that they are desirous of appropriating the funds belonging to the said school to the benefit, support and maintenance of Saint John's College, in such manner as shall be consistent with, and better fulfil the intentions of the founders and benefactors of the said school, in advancing

the interests of piety and learning, and have prayed that
a law may pass for the said purpose," wherefore the
second section of the Act, immediately following the preamble, enacts that, the prayer be granted and that, upon
the mutual agreement of the parties upon terms, "all
the lands, chattels, and choses in action and property"
belonging to the said school may be conveyed by deed to
the Visitors and Governors of St. John's College.

The third section enacts that if such conveyance be
not effected, the property shall remain in, or revert to,
the Rector, Governors, Trustees and Visitors of King
William's School, who are, in said section, incorporated,
with power to carry out the original purpose of the school,
by the name of the Rector and Visitors of Annapolis
School, and by no other name to be known.

The subscriptions obtained for St. John's College under
the above mentioned provisions of law, prior to 1786,
from other sources than the State's Treasury, had thus
amounted to the sum of eleven thousand pounds sterling,
including two thousand pounds subscribed under the legal
provisions already narrated, by King William's School.
This sum entitled the Rector and Visitors of said school,
by the terms of St. John's charter, to elect two Visitors
and Governors, who were accordingly elected as members
of the original Board, at a subscribers' meeting held in
1784—nine other members being elected, one by each
subscriber, or class of subscribers, of one thousand pounds.
The first meeting of this Board of Visitors and Governors
elected by the subscribers was held February 28, 1786,
and the following named members duly qualified on that
day before one of the Judges of the General Court: Right

Rev. Thomas J. Claggett, D. D., Rev. William West,
D. D., Nicholas Carroll, Esq., John H. Stone, Esq., William Beans, Esq., Richard Ridgely, Esq., Samuel Chase,
Esq., John Thomas, Esq., Thomas Stone, Esq., Alexander C. Hanson, Esq., LL. D., and Thomas Jennings, Esq.,
the last two elected by the Rector and Visitors of King
William's School. On the first day of March, 1786, this
Board of Visitors and Governors fixed upon Annapolis
as a place proper for establishing the College—nine votes
being cast in favor of this location and but two in favor
of Upper Marlborough—the only other place considered.
At the same time, the consolidation of King William's
School and St. John's College was carried into practical
effect by the transfer of its property to, and merger of its
newly named successor, the "Annapolis School," in, the
college. Subsequently, in 1789, ten members were elected
to their Board by the votes of the Visitors and Governors,
and the succession has been maintained by such elections
of new members to the present time. The names of those
elected, as above mentioned, to the Board of Trustees in
1789 were—Gustavus Brown, M. D., John Allen Thomas,
Charles Carroll of Carrollton, Jeremiah Townley Chase,
Charles Wallace, James Brice, Richard Sprigg, Edward
Gantt, Clement Hill, and Right Rev. John Carroll, D. D.

Annapolis having been thus selected for the site of the
college, by the terms of the seventh section of its charter,
St. John's obtained the grant of "all that four acres of
land within the city of Annapolis, purchased for the use
of the public and conveyed on the second day of October,
seventeen hundred and forty-four, by Stephen Bordley,
Esquire, to Thomas Bladen, Esquire, then Governor, to

have and to hold the said four acres of land with the appertenances to the said visitors and governors, for the only use, benefit and behoof of the college or seminary of universal learning forever."

The charter likewise empowers the Visitors and Governors to acquire other property, both real and personal, and to alienate all such acquisitions, saving and accepting, however, anything acquired by the original charter-grant.

The "appertenances" belonging to this four acres of land consisted of the remains of a handsome mansion, projected by Governor Bladen about 1744, for the official residence of the Colonial Governors, which though commenced under the supervision of a Scotch architect, who came to the country especially to construct it, was never completed for the purposes originally intended, owing, we are told, to a quarrel between the Governor and the Legislature. Hence this building went almost to ruin, and remained uncompleted for years, receiving the popular name of "Bladen's Folly" or "The Governor's Folly." This popular appellation was recorded in verse by a local poet, who, in the Annapolis Gazette of September 5, 1771,—the old church on the site where now stands St. Anne's being sadly in need of repairs,—published some lines on the subject, headed as follows: "To the very worthy and respectable inhabitants of Annapolis, the humble petition of their old church sheweth."

The old church is made to speak in the first person and in the course of the "petition" says:—

"With grief in yonder field, hard bye,
A sister ruin I espy:—
Old Bladen's palace, once so famed,
And now too well 'the folly' named,
Her roof all tottering to decay.
Her walls a-mouldering all away."

It is needless to add that on the present "College Green" or campus stands the "Governor's Folly," near whose walls, since crowned by "McDowell Hall," we are now assembled.

On the 10th of March, 1786, it was resolved by the Visitors and Governors to repair and finish this old structure and to add wings on the North and South sides and a building-committee was appointed consisting of Alexander Contee Hanson, Nicholas Carroll and Richard Ridgely, Esquires, to carry into effect such a plan. The building, however, was completed, without these additions, in its present form and style, and it is said that the marks indicating the lines of union between new and old work in making repairs and completing the walls, are still visible.

On the 11th of August, 1789, at a meeting of the Visitors and Governors, "Bishop Carroll was unanimously elected President of the Board," and "Dr. John McDowell appeared and accepted the professorship of Mathematics, tendered him on the 14th of May preceding." The Rev. Ralph Higginbottom, then Rector of St. Anne's Parish, "was also elected professor of Languages" at this meeting.

The college-building having been made habitable, the "11th day of November, 1789, was selected for the occasion of opening the Institution, and the Rev. Dr. Smith was requested to attend as Principal of the College, *pro tempore*, and to deliver a sermon. The dedication was performed with much solemnity, all the public bodies, (state and municipal, and citizens and students), being in attendance, and forming a long procession from the State house to the College Hall." An address, on the "Advantages of a classical education," was also delivered by the Rev. Ralph Higginbottom in addition to the sermon preached by the Rev. William Smith. On this occasion, Charles Carroll of Carrollton, appeared, qualified as a Visitor and Governor, and took part in the proceedings of the day.

With Dr. John McDowell, LL. D., as Professor of Mathematics, now presiding as Principal, and Rev. Ralph Higginbottom, Professor of Languages, the College started into life. Mr. Higginbottom brought with him many scholars from King William's and the Annapolis School, of which he was the last Head Master.

On May 14th, 1790, Dr. McDowell was elected by the Board Principal of the College, efforts to obtain a Principal from England having, up to that time, failed of response; and in the same year, a Professor of grammar, Patrick McGrath, was added to the faculty. On November 10th of this year a convocation, composed of representatives from Washington and St. John's Colleges was held at Annapolis before the Governor of the State, as Chancellor *ex officio* of "The University of Maryland," as provided in section 23 of St. John's Charter, already quoted, the purpose in view being the union of both Colleges under the title of said University. This union, it is needless to add, has never been consummated, though

in May, 1791, representatives from St. John's appeared
at another convocation at Annapolis, at which Washington College was not represented. The Chancellor thereupon adjourned the convocation to "the second Wednesday in November next," and no more convocations appear
to have been held. The causes which prevented the consummation of this union it would not be profitable here
to discuss. The spirit and temper of the times, influ-
enced doubtless by the lack of facilities of travel, had inaugurated the plan of two Colleges, as a compromise
between conflicting views and interests, and thus both
energy and means were spent to less, instead of greater
advantage. In 1792, Mr. Higginbottom was made Vice-
Principal by the Board; and "the sum of 275 lbs. was
expended for the purchase in London of the requisite
Philosophical apparatus," and by the succeeding year,
three additional teachers had been added, making a corps
of six professors including the Principal and Vice-Principal.

In 1793, at its first Commencement, St. John's conferred the degree of B. A. upon three graduates, Charles
Alexander, John Addison Carr and William Long, but
the alumni, credited to this class, number in all sixteen,
of which number one became Governor of the State; one,
a Judge of the Court of Appeals; two, Associate Judges
of a judicial district; one, the Clerk of the Executive
Council; one, a Register of Wills; and one, a Visitor and
Governor of the College. The Historical Society of Anne
Arundel County is authority for the following, to say the
least, remarkable summary of the earlier work of St.
John's:

"From its first Commencement, held in 1793, to that of 1806, a brief period of thirteen years, we find among the names of its graduates those of no less than four Governors of Maryland, one Governor of Liberia, seven members of the Executive Council, three United States Senators, five members of the U. S. House of Representatives, four Judges of the Court of Appeals (General Court), eight Judges of other Courts, one Attorney-General of the U. S., one U. S. District Attorney, one Auditor of the U. S. Treasury, six State Senators and fifteen members of the House of Delegates; besides foreign consuls, officers of the Navy and Army, physicians and surgeons, distinguished lawyers, (including a chancellor of South Carolina,) college professors and others."

Among this array of learning and worth it will not be invidious to mention the name of one of the class of 1802, David Hoffman, LL. D., author, historian and jurist, a citizen of Maryland, eminent in his own and a neighboring State, as well as abroad, and upon whom degrees were conferred by the Universities at Oxford and Gottingen. Dr. Hoffman was both a patron and a Visitor and Governor of St. John's.

Of the pupils of St. John's in its early days, the "Maryland Collegian" of March, 1878, states: "We find from an examination of the old matriculating register that between the years 1789 and 1805, it shows not only representatives of every county of Maryland and the City of Baltimore, but also from the States of Pennsylvania, Delaware, Virginia, North Carolina, South Carolina, Georgia and Louisiana. We find there representatives from no less than nine counties of the State of Virginia, and the following well-known Virginia names: Washington, Custis, Dulany, Alexander, Thompson, Clark, Herbert, Lomax, Taylor, Benson, Gibbon, Love, Blackburn, Burwell, Mercer, and others." The same authority finds the names of two students from England; one from France; three from the West Indies; one from Portugal; and, "omitting as many, quite as distinguished," the following Maryland names of Jennings, Dulany, Carroll, Stone, Pinkney, Lloyd, Chase, Ogle, Hanson, Thomas, Murray, Ridgely, Key, Dorsey, Snowden, Harwood, Stewart, Lee and Howard.

The Custis above named among the Virginians refers to George Washington Parke Custis, the stepson and ward of Washington, who, it is said, took a great interest in St. John's, which he manifested by sending there his own ward as a pupil. The genial old gentleman, Mr. Custis, was at one time a member of the class of 1799, and survived long enough to be personally known to several of my brothers alumni present.

Memorable among the distinguished names of graduates during the period above named, stand the names of Francis Scott Key, B. A., and John Shaw, B. A., M. D. They early gave promise of their great talents and usefulness. It is said that Mr. Higginbottom took great pride in exhibiting before visitors the accomplishments of these students and others, who, with them, formed the graduating class of 1796. Mr. Key's talents as a poet were also shared by his classmate, Shaw. The poems of each have been preserved in book form. In 1810 a volume of Dr. Shaw's poems appeared, containing the following sonnet written some years previous and probably

the oldest preserved record, in song, of the old college tree
of pre-historic growth, whose wide-spreading branches,
still living, now wave over this audience :—

"Thee, ancient tree, autumnal storms assail,
   Thy shatter'd branches spread the sound afar;
Thy tall head bows before the rising gale,
   Thy pale leaf flits along the troubled air.
No more thou boastest of thy vernal bloom,
   Thy withered foliage glads the eye no more;
Yet still, thy presence in thy lonely gloom
   A secret pleasure to my soul restore.
For round thy trunk my careless childhood stray'd,
   When fancy led me cheerful o'er the green,
And many a frolic feat beneath thy shade,
   . Far distant days and other suns have seen.
Fond recollection kindles at the view,
   And acts each long departed scene anew."

Dominie Higginbottom is said to have been a graduate
of Trinity College, Dublin, and a complete master of the
Latin and Greek languages. He was ordained a priest of
the established church before emigrating to America. He
resigned the Rectorship of St. Anne's parish, in 1804, but
remained Vice-Principal of St. John's until his death in
1813. Dr. McDowell, and the Faculty under him, thus
gave to St. John's its grand history, until 1806.

On May 12th of said year, the Visitors and Governors
passed a resolution which recited that, "Whereas, by
virtue of an act of the Legislature of Maryland, at their
last session, the donation from the State for St. John's
College of seventeen hundred and fifty pounds per annum,
will cease and determine on the first day of June next,

therefore,—Resolved, that the Principal, Vice-Principal, Professors and Masters of said College be discontinued on the tenth day of August next." The Board of Visitors and Governors, however, notwithstanding this necessary measure, made the best provisions possible for continuing the college work.

Though re-appointed by the Visitors and Governors, this sudden shock to the brilliant usefulness of the college so depressed the health and spirits of Dr. McDowell that he declined re-appointment. Mr. Higginbottom, however, notwithstanding said Resolution, appears to have been retained, and Dr. McDowell was elected a member of the Board of Visitors and Governors. Subsequently he accepted the chair of Provost of the University of Pennsylvania, resigning his office as Visitor and Governor of St. John's. In 1815 he returned to the State, and was again offered the position of Principal of the College. This he declined, and was again made a Visitor and Governor. Dr. McDowell is said to have been "a man of fine presence, and of a pleasing and winning address, combining in a remarkable degree great firmness and dignity of character with an almost feminine gentleness. He was a thorough scholar, and a Christian gentleman, greatly beloved by all who knew him." He died in February, 1821.

Returning to the work of the College, begun and continued under the régime of its succeeding Principals, St. John's history exhibits heroic efforts on the part of its officers and friends to maintain its original high standard of efficiency; and the struggle, though a hard one, has been carried on to success,—very great success, certainly, if the quality, not mere numbers, of the graduates be taken as the standard of comparison; as will appear from the facts yet to be narrated.

Dr. McDowell's successor was the Rev. Bethel Judd, D. D., who was elected in 1807 and remained as Principal until about 1812. The Rev. Mr. Allen, in his Notes, tells us that Dr. Judd "was very much respected in the church * * * and in 1811, in the absence of the Bishop, had presided over the Convention." Mr. Higginbottom dying the next year, the College was left without any elected Principal or Vice-Principal, from about 1813 to 1816, when the Rev. Henry Lyon Davis, D. D., was elected Vice-Principal, and in 1820, Principal, holding the latter office until 1824. Dr. Davis was the father of the brilliant orator, the late Hon. Henry Winter Davis, Representative in Congress from Baltimore City; and Mr. Allen tells us that the father "was a man of much learning, of vigorous mind and of commanding personal stature." Dr. Davis was succeeded by the Rev. William Rafferty, D. D., who held the office of Principal from 1824 until 1831. He was elected Professor of ancient languages in 1819 and Vice-Principal in 1820, which office he held until his promotion in 1824. Dr. Rafferty was a native of Ireland, and, we are told, an accomplished Latin and Greek scholar. He was succeeded in 1831 by the Rev. Hector Humphreys, of whose administration more will be said further on.

Any allusion here, however, to the college faculty of this period would be incomplete without mention of the name of Edward Sparks, M. D., professor of ancient languages for more than thirty years from 1822. Dr. Sparks was a native of Ireland, with marked and some of the best characteristics of his race. He, early in life, married into the Pinkney family. He was Acting Principal, in the absence of that officer, and inclined naturally to strict discipline; but he will be long remembered by many, who came under his tuition, for his thorough familiarity with the Greek and Latin courses.

A part of this time, from the accession of Dr. Judd in 1807, to the close of Dr. Rafferty's incumbency, was the period of St. John's hardest struggle to retain its right to be known by its well-earned title of a college. Stripped in 1806 of its whole revenue derived from the State, as we have seen, it yet sent forth two graduates in 1810, each with the degree of B. A., one of whom subsequently became the first territorial Judge of Florida upon the acquisition of that territory by the United States, and the other lived, and died but a few years since—an octogenerian—in the city where stands his Alma Mater. Alumni and citizens of Annapolis, ye well may dwell a moment upon the memory of Dr. John Ridout. His name and that of his senior—Dr. Dennis Claude, an *alumnus* of 1799, who preceded him in death but a few years—must bring home to many of you, still living, memories of two men—noble specimens of God's noblest work. Dispensing good wherever they came,—"they knew their art but not their trade." Not alone shall their children rise up and call them blessed. Many of us can see, in our mind's eye, these lovable, goodly men, and of each one we may verily say: "He was a man, take him for all in all, I shall not look upon his like again." Dr. Claude belonged to that rare school best described by an anecdote told of the State Treasurer, Mr. George Mackubin, another alumnus of St. John's, of the class of 1806, at whose death Dr. Claude succeeded to the office. When Mr. Mackubin was first tendered this office of Treasurer, he said he could not accept it, consistently with his ideas of propriety, because he was a stockholder in the bank in which the funds of the State had for years been kept on deposit. When urged to accept, as a matter of duty, he promptly sold every share of his stock in that bank before he qualified as custodian of the State's funds. Dr. Claude was a man tall in stature, erect, and of dignified mien, with elegant and courtly manners. His kindly eye was yet as piercing as an eagle's. When a surgeon in the Army, tradition says, he fought a duel with General Winfield Scott, both then young men. A knightly antagonist, truly, for the great soldier, who, as he rode down the line in review of his troops, man and horse of colossal proportions, in full sight of the Mexican forces, is said by one of his officers to have looked the very god of war. General Scott in his Memoirs makes mention of Dr. Claude in kindly terms.

From the next year, 1811, to 1830, inclusive, among the graduates and alumni of St. John's appear names of men distinguished in the State and Nation, and of these, in the order of class-years, the names of Reverdy Johnson, U. S. Senator, Attorney-General of the U. S., and Minister to England; Thomas Stockett Alexander, LL. D.; John Johnson, Chancellor of the State; Hon. Alexander Randall, M. A., Member of Congress and Attorney-General of Maryland; John Henry Alexander, LL. D.; the Right Rev. William Pinkney, LL. D., Episcopal Bishop of the Diocese of Maryland and the District of Columbia; the Hon. William H. Tuck, M. A., Judge of the Court of Appeals of Maryland; and Surgeon Ninian

Pinkney, LL. D., Medical Director, U. S. Navy. The versatile genius of John Henry Alexander, distinguished in the Church, in letters, science and the Muses, who was graduated in 1827, when less than fifteen years of age, has illumined both Europe and America. The mere mention of these names shows that St. John's can boast of more jewels than did Cornelia. The Gracchi were but a single pair, but their Alma Mater, in the persons of the two brothers Johnson, the brothers Alexander, and the brothers Pinkney, has given the State a diadem of brilliants, as a crown forever.

The name of another alumnus must be added to this period, and linked with that of one of the class of 1799. I allude to Judges Nicholas Brewer and Thomas Beale Dorsey—citizens respectively of Annapolis and of the County. Judges Dorsey and Brewer were so long associated on the bench, their faces, for years, were so familiar to the citizens of this judicial circuit, that their names are indissolubly associated together by its bar and citizens. These gentlemen belong among the brightest of the array of jurists of the country. They adorned the bench of their own State—compeers of Marshall, Taney, B. R. Curtis and Story. Judge Dorsey died in 1855, and Judge Brewer like him was gathered to the sleep of the valiant and just, in 1864. The triumvirate of Maryland's judiciary among the older alumni of St. John's would be incomplete without here adding the name of that learned, wise and good man, Judge Alexander Contee Magruder, an alumnus of 1794, a member of the Executive Council, State Senator, and Judge, and Official Reporter, of the Court of Appeals.

During this period of noble work on the part of the College, it appears from a brief sketch of St. John's, published in 1835, that: " In 1821, at a meeting of the Alumni, in the Senate Chamber at Annapolis, a plan of subscription was drawn up, a condition being inserted that the whole should be void, unless the sum of ten thousand dollars should be obtained. Several names were subscribed upon the spot, but no agent was appointed; the requisite sum was not obtained, and the subscription paper has been lost. The only record of it that remains is the payment of the following sum, which was discharged by the donor, though not required to do so by the terms:

" Isaac McKim......... ....$200. ''

But the Rev. Hector Humphreys, D. D., when but thirty-four years of age, was elected Principal of the College in 1831, and held this office until 1857. Largely through his immediate efforts the college was saved to continue its beneficent career, instead of collapsing without further struggle. At the annual commencement in 1832, Dr. Humphreys delivered his inaugural address before the company assembled, and by it inspired the confidence of the public in himself and in his abilities. A confidence which in the course of his career, he more than fulfilled. Brighter prospects immediately dawned upon the college. We are told by Mr. Proud·that to the President's "persevering efforts, and personal influence with members of the Legislature, is also in a great measure to be attributed the Act of Compromise of 1832.'' By this act, the State agreed to add two thousand dollars to the sum of one thousand dollars granted annually in 1811, as heretofore said, and added to the Board of Visitors and Governors, as members *ex-officio*, for the time being, the Governor of the State, the President of the Senate, the Speaker of the House of Delegates, the Chancellor of the State, and the Judges of the Court of Appeals; the Governor being *ex-officio* the President of the Board. The citizens of the State then came bravely to the rescue under Dr. Humphreys' active efforts in St. John's behalf. By a resolution of the Board of Visitors and Governors, adopted February 15th, 1834, the Doctor was appointed with others upon a committee to solicit subscriptions for the benefit of the college, to be applied to the erection of buildings and other improvements. Travelling throughout the State, Dr. Humphreys succeeded in securing about eleven thousand dollars for this purpose, as appears by a long list of subscribers containing the names of many citizens of the State. The large building on the south side of McDowell Hall (since called Humphreys' Hall,) was then erected with these funds and from other carefully husbanded resources, and we are told in the short historic sketch of the College, published in 1835, to which I have before referred and from which I quote, as follows: "The ceremony of laying the Corner Stone was preceded by prayer, by the Rev. Dr. Humphreys, the President of the College. The following inscription, enclosed in a sealed glass vase, was deposited in a metallic box, under the stone: '

'This corner-stone was laid on Thursday, the 18th day of June, A. D., 1835, by the Hon. John Stephen, Presiding Judge in the Court of Appeals, the Rev. Hector Humphreys, D. D., President of St. John's College, and John

Johnson, Esq., one of the Visitors and Governors being present and assisting; His Excellency, Andrew Johnson, being President of the United States; His Excellency James Thomas, being Governor of Maryland, and the Hon. John S. Martin, Thomas Veazey, George C. Washington, Nathaniel F. Williams, and Gwinn Harris, being the Executive Council; and Dr. Dennis Claude being Mayor of Annapolis.

RAMSAY WATERS,
JOHN JOHNSON,   } *Building Committee.'* "
NICHOLAS BREWER, JR.,

Upon this occasion the Presiding Judge of the Court of Appeals made the dedicatory remarks appropriate to the ceremony, and the orator of the day—the Hon. John Johnson (subsequently the last of Maryland's chancellors) made a most forcible and eloquent address. *Nullification* as a remedy for the evils complained of had but recently strained the country to the verge of civil war, but the Chancellor, while expressing thorough belief that the "victims" were honest in their errors, with great perspicuity and force pointed out their *"delusion."* His patriotic address is worthy of a place in the archives of the Nation.

More than twenty years later, August 5, 1857, by resolution of the Alumni Association, the name of Humphreys' Hall was formally conferred upon this building. In the meantime, between 1855 and 1857, the Professors' block of houses was built on the South side of Humphreys' Hall; and Pinkney Hall and the Principal's and Vice-Principal's houses were built on the North side of McDowell

Hall, which about this time had this name formally conferred upon it.

Ably seconded by a faculty consisting of Professors of Ancient Languages, Mathematics, Modern Languages, English studies and of the Grammar Department, with, at times, assistants and tutors in these departments, Dr. Humphreys led a most remarkable career, which has reflected undying credit upon the institution under his charge.

"Hector Humphreys," says Mr. Proud, "was born at Canton, Hartford Co., Connecticut, June 8th, 1797, the youngest member of a family of ten children. His father, George Humphreys, was the fifth of a long-lived family of five sons and five daughters, and held several public offices with credit, having been a Judge of the Court of Probate, and a representative, for nearly twenty years, of his native town in the General Assembly." Dr. Humphreys "entered Yale College a freshman in September, 1814, as one of a class of one hundred * * * and his college course was a succession of triumphs, terminated at the commencement of 1818, by his taking the first honors without a rival, in the estimation of the faculty, or his class-mates, to dispute his claim."

Upon leaving college Dr. Humphreys studied law. "In due course he was admitted to the bar, and opened an office in New Haven, which he occupied for about one year; having received from Gov. Wolcott the appointment of Judge Advocate of the State." Subsequently, circumstances caused him to enter the Episcopal Church and "he was ordained Presbyter, March 6th, 1825, by Bishop Brownell," in the meantime having been a professor of ancient languages in Washington (now Trinity) College, Hartford, "which presided over by Bishop Brownell, numbered among its members the present Bishop Doane of New Jersey, Bishop Horatio Potter of New York, the Rev. Dr. Hawkes and other men of kindred mind and attainments." During this time he had also "officiated with great acceptableness and with marked success, as Rector of St. Luke's Church, Glastonbury, about eight miles from Hartford."

These facts are gathered from Mr. Proud's "Biographical Sketch" of Dr. Humphreys, read at the Annual Commencement of St. John's College August 5, 1857, and published by request of the Association of the Alumni. In this same paper the author referring to Dr. Humphreys' work at St. John's, further states:

"Besides the oral and experimental lectures elicited by the daily recitations, there were stated courses of written lectures, each one hour in the delivery, illustrating with severe and faithful minuteness the several branches taught. I have seen a list in his own hand-writing of the titles of these lectures, with headings of their varied subjects,—which embraced fourteen in Political Economy, twenty-seven in Latin and Greek Literature, twenty-seven in Chemistry and Geology, thirty-four in Natural Philosophy, and six in Astronomy—making one hundred and eight lectures delivered by him in the regular annual course, besides the several recitations of each day!"

I would be undutiful did I not here add, to that of others, my own testimony to the eminent worth, zeal and wonderful acquirements of this truly pious and remarkable man. As boys in the Grammar Department we all

7

felt a sense of respect, amounting to awe, whenever we chanced to be in Dr. Humphreys' presence. These feelings changed to love and veneration when we came under his instruction. By his exertions and direction was procured a well selected philosophical apparatus, for use in different branches of physics, and a cabinet of minerals, fossils, and shells, and a collection of soils and marls from different parts of the State. He directed the construction and outfit of a very good laboratory, and he was the custodian of the standard instruments of weight and measure belonging to the State, the foundations and cases for which were built under his directions in a basement room of McDowell Hall. He knew not how to be idle. His work, while prodigious, was most painstaking and faithful. In chemistry, besides our recitations from the text-book, and his lectures, he carefully, in our presence, analysed soils, both qualitatively and quantitatively. He instructed us in experimental philosophy, and in practical composition and elocution; and from the most approved treatises of the day, we recited to him in Mineralogy and Geology, Evidences of Christianity, Moral and Intellectual Philosophy, Rhetoric and Logic. Under his instruction we studied Butler's Analogy, Kame's Elements of Criticism, Elementary Political Economy, and Kent's Commentaries on International Law and the Jurisprudence of the United States. He taught us the use of the quadrant and how to find the latitude of a place by a meridian observation, and its longitude by time-sights and the chronometer. He discoursed to us on Astronomy and taught us to use the College telescope, and lectured upon most of the subjects above named, besides instruct-

ing us, in the junior and senior years, in the final courses
of Latin and Greek, in which languages he was deeply
versed, and in the beauties of whose literature he took
great delight. He took care in our case, as was his custom
with all the classes in the *senior* year, to examine the
class in and discourse upon English Grammar, in his
endeavor to supplement a practical acquirement of the
mother-tongue by an intelligent comprehension of its
syntax, fortified by reason and rule.

Dr. Humphreys' presence was commanding. He was
tall of stature, with a noble face, and was possessed of a
deeply sonorous though melodious voice. As a pulpit
orator he was eloquent; and his sermons, always deeply
impressive, were often beautiful in poetic imagery. He
was ever ready to fill the pulpit of an absent brother
minister, or to assist in various local duties of neighboring parishes. Several memorial sermons of rare beauty
were delivered by him upon the deaths of persons of eminent worth in the community. The next to the last
Baccalaureate sermon which he preached was delivered
to the class of '55, in St. Anne's Church. I well recall
the circumstances. He had then lost all of his sons, three
in number, the eldest a graduate of the class of '41,
who subsequently was graduated from West Point and
died at Carlisle Barracks from disease contracted in the
Mexican War. These bereavements were sore trials, and
though bravely borne, served greatly to undermine his
health; and he felt in 1855, that his end was not far off. With
much effort, he delivered the sermon. He had not strength
to compose one specially for the occasion, but delivered
the sermon which he had preached to the class of '41,

of which his son, Lieutenant George S. Humphreys, had been a member, and of which the President of the Board of Visitors and Governors, who has just addressed us, is a surviving member,—the text being: "He taught me also and said unto me, Let thine heart retain my words: keep my commandments and live." (Prov., iv. 4). He concluded this sermon somewhat in these words—"What I said to the class of '41 I have now said to the class of '55." And then having referred to the respective careers of the members of the former class, he added— "and one is not." The congregation present was visibly affected, and amid its profoundest sympathy he pronounced the benediction. Though consciously failing, he presided at the Annual Commencement in 1856, but ere the next Commencement season came, he calmly passed away. His death occurred the 25th of January, 1857, and he sleeps the sleep of the righteous in the beautiful spot hard-bye, whose shores are laved by the same waters that lave the borders of this campus (the scene for so many years of his useful life) ere they mingle with the waters of the classic Severn.

A funeral sermon, appropriately entitled "The Cloud of Witnesses," was delivered the 8th of February, 1857, in St. Anne's Church on the occasion of Dr. Humphreys' death, dedicated to the students of St. John's, by the Rev. Cleland K. Nelson, D. D., then Rector of St. Anne's Parish. This tribute was clothed in beautiful language from the text—"We also are compassed about with so great a cloud of witnesses"—(Hebrews, xii. 1,) and fitly perpetuates the testimony to the exalted character and purity of life of the deceased.

The necrology prepared by Mr. Proud includes the names of a number of alumni graduated during the period of Dr. Humphreys' incumbency, all of pure and upright men; some of great talent and promise ere they passed away. But none purer or more upright than John G. Proud, Jr., of the class of '34, belong to this, or any other period in the history of the College. He died August 28, 1883. His ode to "The old Poplar Tree of the Old College Green" is worthy of a place beside "Woodman, spare that Tree." It was read before a meeting of the alumni, February 22nd, 1852. Its reading inspired John Henry Alexander, impromptu, to compose a sonnet to the old tree, in graceful compliment to Mr. Proud's verse. These classic productions, including Dr. John Shaw's beautiful sonnet, written early in the century, are as deeply impressed in your memories, my brethren of the alumni, as is the old tree itself, now clothed in the exuberant foliage of summer's solstician season. May this old tree long survive to inspire the muse throughout generations yet unborn; and, when its life shall have gone out forever, may its youthful offspring, whose roots now await but the earthy covering which in a few moments will be laid upon them, by the fair hands of the lady who now so graciously presides as Mistress of the Executive Mansion,* then serve as a land-mark to keep alive and green for other spans of years the memory of the old tree and its legendary history.

The record, for this same period, of those living gives us the names of upright and talented occupants of the

---

* Mrs. Jackson, wife of the Governor of Maryland.

pulpit and bench, members of the bar, officers of State-governments, and of the Army and Navy.

The Rev. Cleland K. Nelson, D. D., worthily succeeded Dr. Humphreys, and assuming the office of Principal of the College in 1857, retained the chair until 1861. A class was graduated under his régime in each of the years 1857, 1858, 1859 and 1860. The Law, Medicine, the State, the Church, the Army and the Navy, and the Congress of the United States claims each a fair proportion of the number of these graduates, about one-half of whom have had the degree of M. A. conferred upon them by their Alma Mater.

And now comes a decade, half of which may be but passingly alluded to, in which St. John's conferred no degree, nor sent forth from its portals a graduate. Grim visaged-war raged and, unlike at the Temple of Janus, the doors of St. John's were closed. Of its youth thence departing, some—their warfare o'er—

> "Dream of fighting fields no more,
> Days of danger, nights of waking."

Maryland lay on the border-line of the conflicting forces. The dogs of war, once let loose, it was practically all one way North, it was all one way South. But in the border-commonwealths, literally brother was arrayed against brother, father against son, and son against father. And even tenderer, the tenderest of all ties, were severed. The Naval Academy, a school wherein is taught the art of war, was removed from Annapolis, out of sound of hostile cannons' roar, that its novices might study the rudiments of their profession, undisturbed by war's alarms; and the grounds and buildings of St. John's, as well as those of the Naval Academy, were devoted by the Government, as hospitals, to the shelter and care of sickness and suffering. The Florence Nightingale of America came with her ministering spirits and soothed the sorrows of the dying, or nursed others to health and strength, only to return again to scenes of carnage.

But smiling peace again her gentle reign restored. And may the portals of St. John's, then reopened to fair learning's sway, never again close, in either peace or war.

Before taking up the new history of St. John's, subsequent to the suspension of its functions as a College,—though during such suspension, a school was maintained by the Principal of its Grammar Department, Professor William H. Thompson, M. A., an alumnus of the class of '38, by virtue of its chartered rights and the authority of its Visitors and Governors—some short account may be given of its Literary Societies, the Theta, Delta, Phi, and the Everett, and of some of the more noted addresses delivered on Commencement days and on other occasions during the *ante-bellum* period.

February 22nd, 1827, Francis Scott Key delivered an address before the Association of the Alumni and the company assembled. It is needless to add that, aside from its other merits, it expressed the depth of his love and veneration for his Alma Mater, in terms becoming the nature and abilities of its author. Upon a similar occasion, February 22nd of the following year, the Hon. John C. Herbert, B. A., of Maryland, of the class of 1794, delivered an address of great philosophic force, and in language most felicitous and chaste. The inaugural address of Dr. Humphreys, in 1832, and Hon. John Johnson's address, in 1835, upon the occasion of the laying of the Corner Stone of Humphreys Hall, have already been referred to.

On July 4th, 1837, Thomas Holme Hagner, M. A., of the class of '35, a native of the District of Columbia, and then a student of law in Annapolis, delivered an address, accompanied by the reading of the Declaration of Independence, before the Theta, Delta, Phi Society. Upon perusal, this address, coming from a recent graduate, yet pursuing his legal studies, cannot fail to strike the reader as phenomenal. In its display of historic and philosophic knowledge, and extent of legal research, in its cogency of reasoning, beauty of diction and fire of patriotism, it is a deliverance which one would suppose could only have been the product of the highest intellectual gifts, at the height of maturity. The College necrology tells us that he died the 26th of March, 1848, indefatigable in his work as Chairman of the Judiciary Committee in the first State Legislature of Florida. His adopted State lost a counsellor, in his early death, at a time when such men could least be spared.

On the 22nd of February, 1842, the Hon. John Tayloe Lomax of Virginia, an alumnus of the class of 1797, delivered an address of great beauty, re-echoing the sentiments expressed by his brother collegian, Key, to whom he feelingly alluded.

At one of its meetings, held in 1845, or 1846, by the Theta, Delta, Phi, Society, which had been inaugurated about 1832, some of its members became somewhat hilarious, we are told; so much so as to bring into the midst of the meeting, from his residence in McDowell Hall, the

venerable form of Dr. Humphreys. Calling the meeting
to order, the Principal, or President as he was commonly
called, addressed it thus: "Young gentlemen, this meeting stands adjourned *sine die.*" It is superfluous, perhaps,
to add that the Theta, Delta, Phi, did then and there
adjourn *sine die*, and, as a Society, was known no more.
Some students, upon a former occasion, were assembled
in the Commons, at a convivial meeting, so said tradition
when I was at College, whereat they became so boisterous
as to bring upon the scene the same dignified person. As
he opened the door, one of the students rose, and amid
the silence of the awe-stricken crowd, looking the "President" straight in the eye, exclaimed—

> " Hector, Hector, son of Priam,
>   Did you ever see a man *as drunk as I am ?* "

The ready wit of the speaker, showing that perhaps the
condition of himself and the others was not so bad as feared,
probably caused the forgiveness of all; for it is not told
that any punishments followed. The youthful hero of
this anecdote, afterwards served his country, with credit,
in the Mexican War. He bears a distinguished name and
has been awarded its highest honors by his native State.
He is now known as a man of affairs among the men of the
country.

On the 22nd of February, 1849, the Hon. Wm. H. Tuck,
M. A., of the class of '27, delivered an address bearing
much on the educational problem and requirements of the
times. This address was marked by the Judge's well
known great analytic powers and legal acumen, and by

a carefully studied statistical review of the subject under consideration.

On the 22nd of February, 1850, the Hon. Alexander Randall, M. A., of the class of '22, delivered an address largely bearing, with prophetic warning, upon the war-cloud, then no bigger than a man's hand—the compromise measures of 1850 then pending before Congress. With great force, the treasures of the Union, as set forth by the Father of his Country, and the great men of the nation, and the moral of the Roman fasces, illustrated in the national motto, "E Pluribus Unum," were brought before the assembled company of students, alumni and citizens, the address concluding with the verse:—

" Then conquer we must, when our cause it is just,
And this be our motto,—'In God is our trust,'
And the Star Spangled Banner in triumph shall wave
O'er the land of the free and the home of the brave ! "

But a few years since (June 14, 1877) passed the centennial day of the adoption of that Star Spangled Banner by Congress, one hundred and twelve years ago this month, in substantially the present form, the stars and stripes numbering thirteen of each. In 1794, by resolution of Congress, the stripes as well as stars were made to number fifteen, then the number of States. But in 1818 the stripes were reduced, by resolution of Congress, to thirteen, and provision was made to increase the stars to the number of States as new States should be admitted into the Union. May we not here well recall, with those words of Key above quoted, the following lines in that familiar apotheosis composed by the youthful Joseph Rodman

Drake, collaborator with Bryant and Halleck in their early days, and author of "The Culprit Fay" :—

> " Flag of the free, heart's hope, heart's home,
>   By angel-hands to valor given,
> Thy stars have lit the welkin dome,
>   And all thy hues were born of heaven.
> Forever float that standard sheet,
>   Where breathes the foe but falls before us,
> With freedom's soil beneath our feet
>   And freedom's banner floating o'er us! "

The Legislature of Maryland, at its last session, appropriated a sum of money to assist the "Francis Scott Key Monument Association" in erecting a monument to Key's memory, in the further adornment of the Monumental City. May the Congress of the United States not longer defer the erection of a tomb to mark the spot in Frederick City where lie the remains of the Nation's patriot and poet.

On the Commencement days of February 23d, 1852, February 22nd, 1855, and August 6th, 1856, addresses were delivered respectively by the Rev. William Pinkney, Dr. Ninian Pinkney, and Dr. Russell Trevett, Professor of Ancient Languages at St. John's. It is unnecessary to say more of these addresses than that they bore the stamp of the men—the erudition and graceful and poetic language of the Bishop; the native oratorical force of the Surgeon; and the cultivation and classic lore of the Professor.

The Everett Literary Society took its rise about 1857, but terminated its existence in 1861.

Turning now to the Phœnix—St. John's of 1866—its Visitors and Governors, obtaining the means and encouragement voted to it in that year by the Legislature, as heretofore told, elected Henry Barnard, LL. D., then but recently the U. S. Commissioner of Education, Principal of the College. Dr. Barnard organized its several departments anew, and with a preparatory department, a freshman class and a faculty of professors, St. John's again engaged in the educational work of making men and scholars of the youth in its charge. Dr. Barnard had travelled over the State, making interest for the College, and was very active in his efforts to restore it to fame, but after opening the College, in September, 1866, he remained in office less than a year, resigning in the following summer. He is now residing at Hartford, Connecticut.

Dr. James C. Welling, LL. D., succeeded Dr. Barnard, as Principal, and the College-term opened in September, 1867, under his charge, with one hundred and fifteen students. Dr. Welling resigned in 1870, and has held, for years, the chair of President of Columbian University. Under his administration no class was graduated from St. John's, but the junior class completed its junior year. That Dr. Welling's administration was eminently efficient and successful we have the testimony, than which none could be higher, of Professor Hiram Corson, LL. D., of Cornell University, who tells us, in an address delivered on the 7th of July, 1875, at the annual Commencement on that day at St. John's, that, "a great impulse was imparted to the prosperity of the College, by the faithful and energetic administration of Dr. Welling." He adds: "When he resigned * * * the college had made a great move forward in the scholarship of its students, some of whom, now before me, would have done honor to the classes of the best equipped Colleges of the land." Professor Corson was then attached to Cornell, having resigned his professorship of Anglo-Saxon and English Literature and Elocution, held by him at St. John's from 1867 to 1870.

Dr. Welling was succeeded by James M. Garnett, LL. D., in October of the same year, 1870, who held the chair of Principal for ten years. Dr. Garnett's numerous able reports to the General Assembly, his researches into the financial legislation affecting the College and into its general history, and his able farewell address to the students, delivered on Commencement Day, the 30th of June, 1880, all show his devotion to their welfare and to that of the College. A class, each year, was graduated during his whole term of office.

Dr. Garnett was immediately succeeded by the Rev. John McDowell Leavitt, D. D., who continued four years as Principal. A distinguishing feature of his administration was a radical departure from the traditional curriculum of old St. John's. Of the classic sect it had theretofore been of the strictest. Dr. Leavitt organized a Department of Mechanical Engineering, obtained the detail of an Engineer Officer by the Navy Department, as instructor in mathematics and engineering, and started the equipment of a machine shop for practical instruction. He also endeavored to obtain the services of an officer of the Army as instructor in military tactics and other branches of learning necessary to the education of a soldier. This detail, however, came later. A class was graduated during each year of Dr. Leavitt's term of office. Dr. Leavitt thus, before taking his departure, placed St. John's squarely up with the times, and en rapport with the junior institutions of the country which had sprung up with its growth. He resigned in 1884, and now pursues the intellectual delights of literary labor in Brooklyn, N. Y. He has come back to be present to-day with us, and the graceful muse of this scholar among the *literati* of the times will, before we part, sing to us, by request of the Alumni, a poem in commemoration of St. John's One Hundreth natal day.

Upon the departure of Dr. Leavitt, the curriculum of the College was preserved, its interest stoutly maintained, and the duties of Principal performed, by Professor William Hersey Hopkins, M. A., Ph. D., long a faithful professor at the College, and an alumnus of the class of '59. During his term of office an Army officer was added to the corps of professors. Two classes were graduated under the administration of Acting Principal Hopkins, in 1885 and 1886; after which he resigned his position at St. John's to accept the presidency of the Woman's Methodist College in Baltimore, over which he still presides.

Principal Thomas Fell, LL. D., now holds the administration of St. John's, having been elected in 1886, the term-course of that year commencing under his executive authority. His zeal and activity manifested in the conduct of the affairs of the College are well known to you, my brethren of the Alumni, and in particular to those of you who are Visitors and Governors, who are doubtless satisfied that he will take care that your rules are faithfully executed. A class was graduated in 1887, and another in 1888, and to-morrow the class of '89 will be awarded its degrees, leaving college-classes in regular order of succession, and a full corps of professors in its several Departments, including an Army Officer, a graduate of West Point, and an Engineer Officer, a graduate of the Naval Academy. A special Preparatory Department also exists, for the instruction of candidates for entrance to the Naval Academy.

Since the closing of the hiatus in the work of the College in 1866, the sons which St. John's has given to the world have well fulfilled their missions. The Church, the Law and Medicine, and various other departments of human effort and industry have been enriched by their presence and energies. The survivors are yet young enough to reach the summit of their several vocations or ambitions. One of the class of '72 already adorns the Supreme Bench of Baltimore City,* and another, of the class of '73, is an eloquent divine who, as the orator of the day by request of the Alumni, will address you, and upon whose time I fear I have already too long intruded. Another son, Commander Dennis Mullan of the Navy, bearing at the time St. John's honorary degree of M. A., was on duty with his brother heroes in the recent Samoan hurricane, and, of her dead, Lieutenant James Lockwood of the Army, died after extending the "boundary of known land twenty-eight miles nearer the pole," reaching the "most northerly point on land and that ever has been attained by man."

Among notable addresses delivered before the alumni and Philokalian and Philomathean Societies of the College, which Societies were established soon after 1866, are those, in the order of their delivery, of the Hon. Fred-

*Hon. Henry David Harlan.

crick Stone, M. A., of Charles County, July 29th, 1868, an alumnus of '39, and a Judge of the Court of Appeals; the Hon. Geo. Wm. Brown, LL. D., of the Baltimore Bar and Bench, July 27th, 1869; the Rev. Orlando Hutton, D. D., July 27th, 1870, an alumnus of '34; Dr. James C. Welling, July 25th, 1871; the Hon. Alexander B. Hagner, a son of Princeton upon whom St. John's has conferred the degree of LL. D., July 30th, 1872; Surgeon Ninian Pinkney, July 29th, 1873; the Hon. Andrew G. Chapman, M. A., of Charles County, July 30th, 1873, an alumnus of '58; a Baccalaureate sermon delivered by the Rev. Thomas U. Dudley, D. D., June 28th, 1874, of Christ Church, Baltimore, now Bishop of Kentucky; the address of Professor Hiram Corson, above referred to, July 7th, 1875; the farewell address of Dr. Garnett, before referred to, June 30th, 1880; and an address by Dr. Leavitt, on the "Engine, Anvil, Lathe and Foundry," delivered the 15th of June, 1881.

Of various Reports, Memorials, and other papers prepared at different times, by the Board of Visitors and Governors, officers of the college and others, addressed to the citizens of the State and the General Assembly, time does not suffice to make special mention. Much of the matter therein contained has been condensed in these pages. But a moment's time may be spared here to make brief reference, in particular to the addresses, in the list above given, of Dr. Welling and the Hon. Alex. B. Hagner, Associate Judge of the Supreme Court of the District of Columbia. That of Dr. Welling, entitled "The Communion of Scholars, Visible and Invisible," delivered before the Philokalian and Philomathean Societies, was not only brimming with classic lore, but sparkled with originality, native wit, and expressions of good fellowship with his brethren of the communion. Judge Hagner's address before the same Societies, touching, in our day, "the universal diffusion of knowledge among men," stamped the effort as the production of the scholar-jurist, versed in science and literature, not alone pertaining to his profession, while at the same time possessed of those other accomplishments which impart dignity to the law, through the persons of its expounders, and compel respect and obedience to its majesty.

Its Register shows that since the year 1830, St. John's has conferred the honorary degree of D. D. upon seventeen distinguished divines, and the honorary degree of LL. D. upon twenty-four scholars, men eminent in the State and Nation, in addition to the various degrees conferred upon its own graduates, since the year 1793.

The College Library, many years since, was enriched by additions to its shelves, by bequest of Lewis Neth, of Annapolis, an alumnus of 1806, and a few years since by the gift of valuable works by Dr. Thomas B. Wilson, of Philadelphia. Additions are carefully made, as means will permit, and its shelves now contain about six thousand volumes.

Mention must not be neglected of the important adjuncts pertaining to athletics. The Gymnasium and the Boat Club now supplement the Base-ball Nine and the Foot Ball Team, and St. John's cannot be defeated in any competitive exhibition where prizes are given for the *mens sana in corpore sano.*

My attempt to outline St. John's history now rounds
out its hundred years of chartered existence as a College,
and brings its career down to the exercises of to-day, in
commemoration of its Centenary. Briefly now contrast
the limited environment of St. John's in 1789 with its
present environment:—

In the first place, we are struck with this instance of
history repeating itself in a certain round of events.
Under Queen Anne we have seen King William's School
organized, and subsequently transmute itself, under a
Master from Dublin University, into St. John's College,
transferring both Master and Pupils. To-day, under
Queen Victoria, London University supplies St. John's
with its Principal. If Massachusetts sent to the Puritan
men of Severn missionaries to instruct them in their
religious duties, prior to the birth of St. John's, to-day
St. John's supplies one of Boston's pulpits with an alumnus of '73,* our orator of the day, whose learning and
eloquence were his passports to his call to the Athens of
America. Thus linked through time as Boston and Annapolis are, the following beautiful passage from Bishop
Pinkney's address, before referred to, seems particularly
appropriate to be repeated here:

"It is said that Boston is eloquent in incident and association; and he must be dead to the beauty and power of
all that is rich in incident and thrilling in circumstance,
who does not concede the justice of the high eulogium.
But Boston is not a whit more eloquent in those mighty
springs of human action than Annapolis. If the tea-ex-
ploit of one wakes the patriot bosom of her youth to high

*Rev. Leighton Parks, M. A., Rector of Emmanuel Church, Boston.

enthusiasm, the other boasts of a like illustrious exploit.
If Washington blew the first bugle blast of freedom on
Boston heights, and unsheathed beneath the old American
Elm the sword that was to win his country's freedom,—
it was in Annapolis he returned it to its scabbard without one dishonoring stain upon it, when that country's
freedom was achieved. Oh, then, do you not see that he
who would address you on an occasion like the present
must sink his own personal insignificance in the glory
and grandeur that everywhere surround him. 'The past
is secure.' It can never perish—It is written on the page
of history.

"When that page is closed and men cease to read it
with delight, then, indeed, will national exaltation be a
dream and freedom live but in name."

When the College first opened its doors the stage-coach
and sail-packet were the only public means of travel
known, and the horse the only "limited express." To-
day not only can three thousand miles of ocean be crossed
in six days by steamship, but the sub-marine telegraph
has well nigh encircled the globe, and London, New York
and China converse by means of a wire and code of signs,
with the speed of electricity. And persons may converse
together in articulate speech by means of a wire uniting
places one hundred miles distant. The cost of developing steamship power by the combustion of coal has decreased within the last forty years more than one-half,
while the speed of the ship has been nearly doubled. A
consumption of fully four pounds of coal per horse power
per hour has been decreased to a consumption now of
within two pounds per horse power per hour, and the

speed has been increased from about twelve geographical miles per hour then, to twenty geographical miles per hour now, with this latter reduced consumption of coal. These achievements are significant far in excess of the mere numerical values mentioned. The transmitting and receiving instruments of the electric telegraph remained in all essentials the same as those used by Professor Morse when Miss Ellsworth dictated the words—"What hath God wrought!" sent over the first telegraph line constructed in 1844, from Washington to Baltimore, until it occurred to Philip Reis and others that a transmitting instrument sufficiently sensitive might be operated by the air set in motion by vocal and other sounds, instead of by the hand, and by thus effecting the alternate opening and closing of the "electric circuit" to transmit to a receiving instrument sufficiently sensitive, vibrations (similar to those imparted to the transmitting instrument) the air waves produced by which, acting upon the ear, would there resolve themselves into the same sounds as those transmitted. Reis and others succeeded in so transmitting vocal and some other sounds, but not human speech. It remained for Professor A. Graham Bell, encouraged, in pursuing his investigations, by Professor Joseph Henry (to whom the world is indebted for the invention of the electro-magnetic telegraph) to declare, in about the year 1876, the law, and show the error which had confronted Reis and others. Bell demonstrated graphically and by written description, that articulate speech could only be transmitted over a "closed circuit;" not by making and breaking the electric circuit, as is done in telegraphing sounds or signs, and which was the theory upon which Reiş and others sought the accomplishment of transmitting articulate speech, and failed. The mystery solved by Bell's discovery, scientific and other mechanics soon improved Bell's primitive instruments, a notable improvement being the carbon-transmitter, the invention of Mr. Thomas A. Edison, the electrician of world-wide fame. Passing by any mention, except by name, of the locomotive, which supplanted the stage-coach, and of the phonograph, graphophone, electric motors and dynamos, the latter being now the rival of the gas-light plant, we are confronted with the questions: What next—and what is to be the outcome of these marvels in science and art developed into practical inventions? The university, the college, and the workshop have wrought these changes, in the past century, and a condition of humanity consequent thereupon,—to some thinkers a disastrous condition. From its Greek text Professor Corson in his comprehensive and masterly address, heretofore mentioned, quotes a beautiful translation in the following sentence:

"Unfortunately for the intuition of this age, its materialism and its positivism have induced 'a condition of humanity which has thrown itself wholly on its intellect and its genius in physics, and has done marvels in material science and invention, but at the expense of the interior divinity.' "

But the Professor does not at all despair of the preservation of the interior divinity. Indeed he supplies in his own words an antidote to the danger of any such destruction, beautifully expressed in the following language:

"There is a time better than any other, in a human life, for the exercise of intuitive instinct, sensibility, emotion, imagination, and a time for the exercise of the analytic and discursive faculties—a time to *feel* the True, the Beautiful and the Good, and a time to regard all these under intellectual relations.

"Now, it is in mistaking times and seasons, in running counter to the processes of Nature's growth, that a teacher of the young may do a great wrong, while honestly and conscientiously endeavoring to do a great good. If, as is too often the case, he force upon young minds instruction in the form of abstract principles, and thus violently tear open the closed bud of reason, not yet ready to be unfolded, instead of bringing to bear upon this tender bud the genial warmth of sensibility, sympathy, and enthusiasm, and thus allowing it to open in its own good season, he does a wrong which can never, in this world, be righted, he inflicts a wound which no time will heal."

Sensibility, sympathy, and enthusiasm, continues Professor Corson, "are the elements of the soil and the atmosphere in which the intellectual, the moral, and the religious nature of a child can alone germinate and grow, and in later years bloom and shed a wholesome fragrance;" and he contends, that these elements are to be developed and brought most effectually into play "only through *concrete* representations of the True, the Beautiful and the Good;—not through an abstract enunciation of principles, not through a code of rules and a system of teaching."

But is there not left safety for the interior divinity while yet the art preservative of arts shall preserve these words for adult ears, addressed to the vulcanic deity of the village smithy?—

> "Thanks, thanks to thee, my worthy friend,
>   For the lesson thou hast taught;
> Thus at the flaming forge of life
>   Our fortunes must be wrought;
> Thus on its sounding anvil shaped
>   Each burning deed and thought."

And yet while university, school and workshop shall graduate an Alexander L. Holley, who, prepared for the classical course at Yale, was then, to use a mechanical term, more English than American, "shunted" therefrom to the scientific course at Brown University, whence he stepped for a year upon the footboards of the locomotive. The "thoughtful locomotive driver" Holley thus describes:—"He is clothed upon, not with, the mere machinery of a larger organism, but with all the attributes except volition of a power superior to his own. Every faculty is stimulated and every sense exalted. An unusual sound amid the roaring exhaust and the clattering wheels tells him instantly the place and degree of danger, as would a pain in his own flesh, * * * a peculiar smell of burning * * *, a cutting valve, a slipped eccentric, a hot journal, high water, low water, or failing steam; these sensations, as it were, of his outer body, become so intermingled with the sensations of his inner body, that this wheeled and fire-feeding man *feels* rather than perceives the varying stresses upon his mighty organism."

Or while the late Prof. E. L. Youmans can be read to say:—

" The star-suns of the remoter galaxies dart their radiations across the universe; and although the distances are so profound that hundreds of centuries have been required to traverse them, the impulses of force enter the eye and impressing an atomic change upon the nerve, give origin to the sense of sight. Star and nerve-tissue are parts of the same system—stellar and nervous forces are correlated. Nay, sensation awakens thought and kindles emotion, so that this wondrous dynamic chain binds into living unity the realms of matter and mind through measureless amplitudes of space and time. And if these high realities are but faint and fitful glimpses which science has obtained in the dim dawn of discovery, what must be the glories of the coming day ? "

Or yet the genius of Bulwer be heard to exclaim:—

" All the genius of the past is in the atmosphere we breathe at present. But who shall resolve to each individual star its own rays of the heat and the light whose effects are *felt* by all, whose nature is *defined* by none. This much at least we know ; that in heat the tendency to equilibrium is constant; that in light the rays cross each other in all directions yet never interfere the one with the other. * * * I say not with Descartes ' I think, therefore I am '—rather ' I am, therefore I think; I think, therefore I shall be.' "

Nor while the sailor (few seafaring men but have poetic temperaments more or less developed by their environment)—the officer in command of an American man-of-war,* could thus indite his heart's lay from the Indian Ocean to his antipodal home:—

* Capt. Townshend commanding U. S. S. Wachusett. He did not live to reach home but died on this cruise.

"My own dear wife, dear boy, dear girls,
　The wealth of love ye bear to me
Is richer than the fairest pearls
　That glisten 'neath this Indian sea;
For gathered 'round our simple hearth,
　Breathing that atmosphere of love,
I'd ask no purer heaven on earth,
　Nor dream a happier heaven above.

Yet far away my treasure lies
　While storm-swept oceans roll between,
The pole-star reigning o'er those skies
　Ne'er gazes on this alien scene;
But as I pace the midnight deck,
　The Southern Cross is blazing high;
Ah! heart estranged, I little reck
　The splendors of this austral sky.
　　　*　　*　　*　　*　　*　　*　　*
Vice-gerent of the God of light,
　I cannot wonder that of old
The Magi worshipped, as the night
　Fled vanquished by thine orb of gold;
Our purer faith, our hopes God-given,
　Feel thy benignant influence still,
Raising each earth-bound soul toward heaven.
　Scattering each brooding fear of ill."

And though the late Professor John W. Draper attributes European civilization to the superiority of the analytic quality of mind, as distinguished from the synthetic of the Oriental, telling us that: "to the work of him who pulls to pieces there is no end, but he who puts things together comes to an end of his task"; yet in contrasting the Pantheistic with the Anthropomorphic belief, he also says:—"the pantheistic is a grand but cold philosophical idea; the anthropomorphic embodies our recollections, and restores to us our dead. The one is the dream of the intellect, the other is the hope of the heart."

Prohibited by its charter from inculcating any form of religious worship, St. John's has ever sought by its every teaching and association, not only to conserve the interior divinity but to teach each student as a man "to carry his own sovereignty under his hat," in the possession of the principles of virtue and patriotism. Within her walls in my class-time, we were all made familiar with the eloquence, and appeals for governmental justice, of Chatham, Burke and Grattan; with the force, beauty and patriotic fire of the words of James Otis, Patrick Henry, William Wirt, Andrew Jackson, Henry Clay and Daniel Webster; and with the noble diction of the solemn warnings of the Father of his Country, who in yonder tall edifice laid his soldier trappings down. Recalling the recent outpouring of the people to swell the grand pageant in New York City, commemorative of the Centenary of Washington's Inauguration on the 30th of April, 1789, we are forcibly reminded of the former event here, when on the 23rd of December, 1783, he returned his Military Commission into the hands of his countrymen. In the words of an English poetess:—

" He saved his land, but did not lay his soldier trappings down,
   To change them for a regal vest, and don a kingly crown,
   Fame was too earnest in her joy—too proud of such a son—
   To let a robe and title mask her noble Washington."

And now at the close of the Centenary of St. John's what of its future? It is not the part of wisdom to look

mournfully into the mistakes of the past committed not
by, but against the College. The munificence of an Anne
Arundel boy, grown to a merchant prince in the commercial metropolis of the State, sent forth in that metropolis
scarce more than a decade since, the Johns Hopkins University, like Pallas from the brain of Jove, full armed for
its work. John McDonogh and George Peabody, the one
a native, and the other an adopted citizen of the State for
many years, have enriched the educational forces of the
people by monumental endowments. May not the citizens
of Maryland, through their representatives in the General Assembly, in conjunction with the Visitors and Governors, now wisely seek to devise plans for making St.
John's absolutely free to the sons of all residents of the
State, board and lodging of the students—non-residents
of the city—being supplied at cost. If then there remained room for more students than the State supplied,
it might well be considered, whether it would not be good
policy to invite free, students from without the State.
The invitation, in view of St. John's location, might well
bear the words—" *Si quaeris peninsulam amoenam circum-
spice*"—the motto of the beautiful State on the borders
of Lake Superior, which so lavishly endows its great free
University. St. John's would thus ever continue on in
fulfilment of Maryland's motto, *crescite et multiplicamini*,
and if not the great University of the State, it would be
to it or to other Universities what the St. John's of Oxford and the St. John's of Cambridge are to those great
Universities. Its roll of students must then of necessity
increase, though, within limits, the cost of few or many
scholars would be the same, and the advantages if too few

rather than too many scholars, would be all in favor of the student's more thorough instruction. The Oxford calendar for 1888, as appears by Whitaker's Almanac for 1889, shows but 122 under-graduates credited to St. John's College, and the average of the twenty-one colleges (excluding the Halls), is 125, the annual income of St. John's being 12,743 pounds sterling, which is near the average income of each of the other colleges. By the same authority, St. John's at Cambridge is credited on the Cambridge Calender for 1888 with 290 under-graduates, the average of the seventeen colleges of the University showing 162, and St. John's gross income being 42,174 pounds.

The College of the City of New York, formerly the New York Free Academy, educates absolutely free and without cost for tuition, books, or use of apparatus, more than a thousand boys and youths, within the city-walls of a single building. The orderly management, the minuteness of detail, the thoroughness of equipment in every Department, from the classical to the workshop, reflect not alone credit upon the President's fatherly and disciplinary care, but upon the faculty, the State and City for furnishing such a boon to many fathers and mothers, as well as to their sons. The good and useful citizens which this institution makes, return, in the production of values, hundreds of times over, all that it costs in taxation for their instruction. It may be that those immediately charged with the responsibility of the supervision of St. John's, legislative and visitorial, might derive some light on State and municipal management of educational institutions by a study of the financial and other management of this College.

The record of St. John's has now been recalled from its beginning. May its record continue on forever. And may its alumni never cease to claim as of old and as of right, entrance into that communion of scholars which cherishes the best thoughts of all time.

Seek you fellowship in temples
Where fair learning holds the key,
Are you challenged at their portals
Ere you enter with the free?
Wave proudly but this legend—
A passport it shall be,—
"My alma mater is St. John's,
'Neath the old historic tree."

In the preparation of this paper, besides the authorities and sources of information named, I have consulted the "Annals of Annapolis," published in 1841, and Riley's History of Annapolis, published in 1887, but, except the Maryland statutes and Reports, I have been unable, for want of time, to consult all the numerous old authorities cited in said publications, and in the Rev. Ethan Allen's Notes, bearing upon Maryland History. I am greatly indebted to Mr. J. Shaaff Stockett, M. A., an alumnus of the class of '44, the Official Reporter of the decisions of the Court of Appeals, for a collection of papers containing *data* of great assistance to me. To Principal Fell; the Hon. Nicholas Brewer, Treasurer of the Board of Visitors and Governors; Daniel R. Randall, Esq., of Annapolis; and Mr. Herbert Noble, of the graduating class, I am much indebted for *data* and courtesies extended. I must also acknowledge obligations to other friends for suggestions; and to Gen. Alexander S. Webb, President of the College of the City of New York, for *data* furnished concerning that institution, and for courtesies extended in furtherance of my efforts to obtain light on my subject.

Pardon, my hearers, this attempt at authorship, which, though willing, is so inadequate to the obligations resting upon me. Were the ability not lacking, the time permissible to the preparation of this paper has been too short to do the subject justice. Though a labor of love, my sketch may be redolent of the shop—even "sounding in tort," as the lawyers say, in abuse of your patience. If this be so, forgive the wrong, but have me enjoined against any repetition of a similar imposition upon your kind attention, for which I am deeply indebted and equally thankful. But if this sketch of our Alma Mater's career shall assist ever so little her merits to disclose, or prove of use to any historian worthy of so noble a theme, then indeed will my labor be requited.

To the young gentlemen of the graduating class who, ere to-morrow's sun shall set, will be numbered in the Alumni Association, I would address a few sentences, more of encouragement than advice. A surfeit of the latter you may have, but it will not put old heads on young shoulders. On this point I am old enough to speak from experience:—

You will find in Bulwer's "Caxtoniana" a mine of great practical advice, expressed in language of his own rare beauty—in which, in one place, he says:—"It is a great thing, said Goethe, to have something in common with the commonalty of men:" and this in addressing dandies, (now called dudes): "Yon sloven, thickshoed and with cravat awry, whose mind, as he hurries by the bow-window at White's, sows each fleeting moment with thoughts which grow, not blossoms for bouquets, but corn-sheaves for garners, will before he is forty, be far more the fashion than you. He is commanding the time out of which you are fading."

While recalling the class motto of 1880, "*Nulla dies sine linea*," do not forget that the famous painter also said, "*ne sutor ultra crepidam.*" The reason of this re-proof and that of the maxim "*ne quid nimis*" may each be considered as but implications of that formula said to be of such "high generality"—the law of von Baer—"The heterogeneous is evolved from the homogeneous by a gradual process of change." Specialize your labor there-fore, if dependent upon it for support. Concentrate your energies, let your culture be never so deep or broad. Choose your life-work, if possible, in that vocation to which you are instinctively led by a taste for it. The rewards of success are far more likely to come under such circumstances, amid the changes and chances of this life. Then you may observe the maxim *age quod agis*, and wisely improving the present, each of you may "go forth to meet the shadowy future without fear and with a manly heart." But remember that, as the poet implored the maiden,—

> "Pausing with reluctant feet,
> Where the brook and river meet,"

to bear on her lips the smile of truth, in her heart the dew of youth,—so your Alma Mater invokes you to a similar course in life. You may not attain to the perfection of ideal femininity; for, the fibres in man's structural organization are of grosser grain combined into coarser and less complex muscular and nervous tissues than those of woman. Nature has wrought this difference, for woman's protection, relying, as has been said, on man's magnanimity not to prove recreant to his trust.

I can yet fully sympathize with you if you are now ready to retort, as against all advisers, in the words in one of Bulwer's minor dramas:—

"Oh, how little these middle-aged formalist schemers
Know of us the bold youngsters, half sages, half dreamers.
Sages half, yes, because of the time passing on
Part and parcel are we, they belong to time gone.
Dreamers half, yes, because, in a woman's fair face
We imagine the heaven they seek in a place."

But read and remember what follows:—

"The world's most royal heritage is his—
Who most enjoys, most loves, and most forgives."

THE PRESIDENT then introduced the REV. JOHN McDowELL LEAVITT, D. D. of Brooklyn, New York, a former Principal of St. John's, who delivered the Centennial Ode, written by him for the occasion.

Maryland.

Oh Maryland, my heart returns to thee
So bright, so fair from mountain to the sea!
These eyes have seen thy beauties from the shore
Where meets broad Chesapeake wild ocean's roar.
To where thy graceful summits lift their green,
And Oakland sits enthroned, a mountain-queen.
O'er many lands I've roam'd but which can show
Such varied charms as in thy daughters glow?
And brave and courteous sons, thy soil now grace,
As when colonial manners ruled the place,
And Washington's majestic form was seen—
Incarnate Freedom, moving o'er our green.
Beneath yon tree, in hoary centuries old,
The victor stood whom ages will behold.
Sublime our State House where, his sword laid down
Proclaim'd a country loved more than a crown!
Nor Maryland, in thee from mount to bay
A lovelier spot than greets our eyes to-day!
Yon ivied walls, yon poplar's lofty brow,
Our college green in summer sunlight now,
This pillar'd hall; above, the time-worn dome,
Make our St. John's beloved as we love home.
A Hundred Years now crown its honor'd head!
A Hundred Years! what memories from the dead!
What fears, what hopes, what toils have marked this Scene!
What names we love are in our hearts kept green!
McDowell learn'd here first the mantle wore;
Here Pinkney, Webster's peer, gain'd classic store;
Here caught the fire of eloquence that burn'd,
And law's dry rugged truths to beauty turn'd;
Then left to one his genius and his name
Beneath whose Bishop's robe glow'd friendship's flame,

9

Whose life of faith, whose word of power and love
Approved the man anointed from above.
Where'er our flag shall float, high o'er the mast
While battle thunders 'mid the ocean's blast,
Or, if on land its brilliant colors fly
O'er patriot warriors taught for it to die,
In peace, in war, above the sailor's grave,
Where'er its banner'd glories flash and wave,
Immortal there, O KEY, shall live thy name,
And our St. John's, thy mother, share thy fame.
But I must pause since thy illustrious men
Need not the pictures of a poet's pen;
They grace the Senate, in the Pulpit shine,
Adorn the Bar, and lead in Mart and Mine,
By Science cure, or ease the pangs of death,
While whispering hope with love's inspiring breath.
Always, St. John's, they grateful turn to thee,
As turns a son to home where'er he be.
Such sober thoughts we leave in pause awhile;
We change our theme and dare the cynic's smile.
We sing of Brass, whose glitter on man's breast
Makes woman's bosom thrill with wild unrest,
And hence our Navy, I'm in whispers told,
With tinsel wins those hearts more prized than gold.
Behind her fan I see the maiden glance;
I see her whirl, clasp'd in the dizzy dance;
She reads her stars, and with an artless joy
An Adm'r'l weds, forsehadow'd in a boy,
Long o'er Life's seas may they together float!
He wears the title; she commands the boat;
He sounds the trumpet; she tells when to blow;
He grasps the helm; she bids him where to go.
When flies the ball across the college field,
By foot or bat, St. John's will never yield;
She takes the laurel from those Naval brows
And her own children with the crown endows.

Thus, Maryland, thou dost bring down the pride
Of ocean-warriors conquering all beside;
And yet, superior thus by nature's hand,
Thou has made void an end by nature plann'd,
And dwarf'd our College, as we soon will show;
Despoil'd our flower of its centennial glow.
Our proof is near and to its light we turn;
Hence o'er our future may new splendors burn!
Where'er our banner streams above the world,
'Mid what wild seas or wars it flies unfurl'd,
There sailor-manhood, taught the waves to rule,
Repays investment in our Naval School.
These young cadets who flirt and dance and joke
Turn heroes 'mid red battles' flame and smoke,
Fight with train'd skill and if they fall to die
In triumph smile as meet our stars the eye.
How grand the proof on far Samoa's shore
When burst across the deep that tempest's roar!
See Mullan, who, to save his ship from wreck,
Dared ocean's tumbling ruin on his deck!
Groans the Vandalia in a death-dark wave
That hurls her martyr-captain to his grave!
Heroic Farquhar bids our banner fly
Out in the storm that mingles sea and sky,
And, as the maniac lightnings flame and glare,
Triumphant music thrills the thundering air!
Hark! Cheers, urge on brave Britons thro' the gloom
Heard o'er the whirlwind's shriek, the billow's boom!
The Trenton and Vandalia crash and shock,
And then with arms of sisters interlock.
That flag, that strain, those shouts wake life again
Where mast and shroud are clutch'd by clinging men.
'Twas thy song's music, KEY, inspired with power
When ocean-demons raged and ruled the hour,
And Maryland, thy spell was felt e'en there,
Since 'twas thy son with hope lit that despair.

Who now will those Samoans dare to grind
Braving both storm and wave their foes to find?
On breast and shoulder those they clasp'd and bore
Whose scorn and bullets they had felt before.
Samoa's Isles, o'er you our Flag shall fly
And the grim tyrants of the earth defy!
Now let me come to my appointed task,
And here a few centennial questions ask!
Love for our college glows!   Why then so poor?
Say, why not yet her name and work secure?
The seed was dropped two centuries ago:
A soil so rich and yet a growth so slow!
In dim colonial times a Hundred Years
'Mid toil and battle, poverty and tears,
Had ample treasure for our college piled;
Hope waved her wings and o'er our future smiled.
The people's gifts accepted by the State
A promise gave of glory, bright and great.
Yes, Maryland, thy honor, hand and name,
Thy seal, thy law, thy pledge, thy truth, thy fame,
All to a TRUST before the world were given;
And to St. John's, thy child, thou bound by Heaven.
Who were the men who gave their work and gold?
A list more brilliant where can earth unfold?
On Freedom's charter read their names in light!
For Freedom's battles they left here to fight;
By pen and sword, by word and blood they show'd
What spark immortal in their bosoms glowed.
The State took gifts of revolution-sires
With halos crown'd flash'd back from war's red fires.
A few years pass!   Lo party storms rage high!
Wild Passion swept with clouds our country's sky!
In our old Hall, for which I love to speak,
A college boy, perhaps in college freak,
A tempest waked—a word of his hurl'd o'er
All that our hero-fathers did before.

By a mere lad enraged the State House frown'd,
And struck a daughter staggering to the ground;
Annull'd her gifts and flung her on the wild,
A bleeding, orphan'd, lone and starvling child.
For thirty years she struggled on the earth
By the stern mother left who gave her birth,
And beggar'd first, was forced by Want to sign
A compact hard, and vested rights resign.
The deed was null! Never can mother bring
Her flesh to pangs, then rob the helpless thing.
No! Maryland! St. John's avoids the deed!
To that mean pact St. John's here "No" doth plead!
Those patriot-gifts, with interest, all are ours;
From THEM the grandeur of our college towers.
We claim a MILLION by eternal right!
A MILLION can be won by faith and fight;
Not to thy courts, but people, our appeal;
Sure, THEY, the wounds their servants gave, will heal.
Now know why Yale and Harvard in the race
Have left St. John's to creep with laggard pace;
Why Princeton and Columbia crowd their halls
While we have round us dim and time stained walls,
Yet, feel like heroes with a battle-scar,
Proud of the wound and limp of noble war.
Yes, Maryland, we come before thee now
Not with a beggar's whine and abject brow
For the sole sum that thou didst then withhold
And paltry interest paid in grudging gold;
We stand on right; we look thee in the face;
We cry—"Wipe out the blot of this disgrace!"
Lift us now up to that illustrious height
Where we *had* shone in this centennial light!
See the cold father who his son denies
The kindly nurtures which love's heart supplies!
That boy to manhood grows, marr'd flesh and soul;
The stamp forever on the shrivell'd scroll;

No gold can paint the cheek with blushing health ;
That shrunken form beyond the power of wealth ;
Thus imbecill'd, what treasure e'er can buy
Strength for the reason, brilliance for the eye ?
A manhood's blight instead of manhood's prime
Is on that father's soul a cloud and crime.
Say, money cannot now the sin repair,
Shall then that father be exempt from care ?
Do nothing since he cannot do the whole,
Or mock his human ruin with a dole ?
No! that hard father shall do all he can,
The boy he blighted comfort in the man.
Oh Maryland, these simple truths apply !
Soon wall and tower will brighten on our sky ;
Soon on our shelves the piling volumes grow ;
The spoils of science we'll be proud to show ;
New telescopes across the stars shall sweep,
New worlds shall glitter in th' aerial deep,
Our honor'd halls shall swarm with noble youth
Panting to drink the life of living Truth ;
Nor Yale, nor Harvard, shall exceed our fame,
While glory brightens round St. John's, thy name !
Why should our youth on others spend their gold ?
Why bear abroad the treasures we should hold ?
Why bloat old colleges with needless wealth
And from our own keep back the bloom of health ?
Why give we other States our sons to guide,
Who trained at home would make our State their pride ?
Stop, Maryland, this drain of thine own blood
For other lives in one centennial flood !
Sons of St. John's ! Your Alma Mater cries !
Kneel at her altars ! Kneel and never rise
'Till each a vow has burn'd into his soul
This dark centennial cloud away to roll !
And you ye daughters of this beauteous place,
Ye, who o'er life can shed such light of grace

Give us your smiles, your words and looks of cheer,
And brilliant triumph yet awaits us here.
Oh Press, for mighty aid we ask thee now,
Fire in thy glance and lightning on thy brow !
Thy pens of flame must light us on our way ;
Thy spell be felt for us from peak to bay !
.The Bar, the Pulpit and each State House Hall,
May eloquence of truth inspire you all !
Him honor'd at our helm may wisdom guide,
And all the noble helpers at his side !
But last and chief our Trustees we invoke
By all their sires and grandsires did and spoke.
Hark ! from the grave the voice of those I hear
Who left this work for an immortal sphere.
Their forms I see ! each reverend face behold !
Back from the past its shadows are unroll'd !
Your fathers cry, all eloquent by death !
The sounds I catch as if from life's last breath !
"Sons, at these altars bend in covenant now,
Make one true, strong, and all uniting vow,
To work and wait, to give and pray and fight
'Till Justice crowns St. John's with her own right !"

At the close of the Poem, Mr. Stockett introduced as the Orator before the Alumni, the Rev. Leighton Parks, M. A., of the Class of '73, Rector of Emmanuel Church, Boston.

The Coming Century.

An invitation to return to one's Alma Mater, to address the Alumni, could be received only with feelings of profound gratitude and surprise. Of gratitude, that the mistakes of the student life had been forgotten ; of surprise that I should have been chosen from the great company of loving sons to speak to such an assembly on such an occasion. I begin without an apology. The invitation of the Alma Mater is like the invitation of the Queen—a command. It is befitting that such be accepted without comment and in the hope that the duty may be faithfully fulfilled.

Were the occasion a less momentous one, the temptation would be great to recall the days that are past, and to ask ourselves, brethren of the Alumni, how far we have fulfilled the expectations of our friends and of ourselves. But if we did would we not be led to say with St. Paul, "Whether there be prophecies they shall fail; whether there be tongues they shall cease; whether there be knowledge, it shall vanish away." The prophecies which we made of one another—of the great deeds some were to do, of the great books others were to write, of the splendid reforms others were to work—they have failed. The stream of eloquence which flowed so smoothly in debate,

we thought would soon widen into the mighty stream of
oratory. It has ceased. The knowledge which we were
so many years in accumulating has almost vanished—
few of us could pass to-day the entrance examinations.
But there is one thing which never faileth—love. Love
for the Alma Mater has drawn us hither to-day. Love
for one another inspires all our greetings, and better
than all, Love of the Beautiful, Philokalians, and Love
of Learning, Philomatheans, grows deeper and stronger
as the years with their mysterious experiences roll over
us.

Our college life then was not a failure. We must
measure ourselves neither by what we have accomplished,
nor by the extent of our reputations, but by a nobler
and higher standard which measures the true man.

> "Not on the vulgar mass
> Called work must sentence pass,
>   *   *   *   *   *   *
> But all the world's course thumb
> And finger failed to plumb,
> So passed in making up the main account;
> All instincts immature,
> All purposes unsure,
> That weighed not as his work, yet swelled the man's amount:
> Thoughts hardly to be packed
> Into a narrow act
> Fancies that broke through language and escaped;
> All I could never be,
> All men ignored in me,
>   This, I was worth to God."*

*Browning's Rabbi Ben Ezra.

The measure of that worthiness is to be found in love. The desire for a pure and noble ideal.

The only question then which we have a right to put to the past is, what have you done to develope in me my proper personality? That is the object of life. If we can ever be right in assigning a final cause to creation, it must be when we say that it was that each individual should be partaker of the Divine nature. That is possible only when the individual realizes that personality which is the manifestation of God.

There are two forces at work for that end. The one is self determinate action of a free spirit and the other the reactive influence of circumstances amid which the individual finds himself. The individual is incapable of realizing his personality in a state of isolation. He attributes his ideal to the Nation, and the Nation, being the embodiment of the manifold personality of the individual members which compose it, possesses power and freedom, wisdom and foresight which does not belong to the individual. The duty of the Nation, that for which it exists, that which leads to its downfall if it fail in its accomplishment, is to return to each individual the larger personality after which he reaches and which he is not able to attain apart from the life of the Nation.

The relation of the individual to the Nation is like that of the leaf to the tree. No matter how great the tree becomes it can always be traced back to the tender leaf which lay curled up in the embryo from which it sprang. And if the time ever comes when the leaves have no opportunity of performing their function the tree dies. The tree is *of* the leaf; it is *by* the leaf; every part, gnarled trunk and waving branch are but the stem and vein of the leaf. It is *for* the leaf, for flaming calix and luscious fruit are but modified forms of the leaf itself which could never have become such a wonder and benefit, in a state of isolation and which the tree exists simply to perfect.

When then we turn our eyes to the Coming Century there is but one question which we wish to put to it, What will you do for Man? And it answers us, look to the Nation and find the answer there.

I. We turn to the Nation first in its *political* aspect. What will the *Government* of the Twentieth Century do for the developement of the Divine Personality in man? What do we want it to do? The men of a hundred years ago, who laid the broad and deep foundations of the Government under which we live, were filled with the love of liberty, no matter what it cost. They defined Government as that which was to exercise the least possible restraint upon the individual, and then only when his acts were found to be injurious to the well being of others. The belief which lay back of all their theories of Government was that each man is capable of indefinite healthy developement, if only he be allowed free scope.

It was a splendid faith in man. And splendidly has it been justified. The intense interest in life which exists in this country is due to that original faith. The curiosity of Americans, which affords so much amusement, is only a crude form of the keen interest in each man's developement, which is possible only in a society in which no one can tell what will be the outcome of the individual's experiences.

Where there is a Paternal Government, half the interest in life is gone, because there is a definite goal to which all life tends by the determination of the ruling power. Who cares to know what two Russian serfs think? If you know what one has accepted as the ideal of life, you have the philosophy which reigns from the Arctic Ocean to the Caspian sea; from the Ural mountains to Poland. The minds of two Chinamen are no less similar than their featureless faces.

This keen interest in life may be the most obvious result of liberty but it is not the most valuable. Independence of Government supervision has begotten a spirit of self reliance which prevents panics or gloomy forebodings. A people who are accustomed to depend upon themselves are not afraid of crises. They do not ask themselves whether some external power will be able to meet the emergency; all they have to consider is whether they and their neighbors are able for it. That confidence which is the result of experience leads them to believe that there will always be found men who will be equal to the occasion. And that faith has been justified. The wonders of Aladdin's Lamp are as nothing to the changes of fortune which have come to men in this country, and found them equal to the new occasion —the son of the Boston tallow chandler at the Court of France, and the Illinois backwoodsman coping with the first Diplomats of Europe, will occur to every one; and may we not add the dignity and gracious courtesy of the late Mistress of the White House? Well, these things are possible only as the result of a boundless liberty which trains men and women to depend upon their innate sense of what is wise and true, rather than to be trammelled by traditional rules of conduct which it requires a life-time to master and a particular caste to perpetuate.

That the people of the United States are, as a whole, more interested, and so more happy—more self reliant and therefore more hopeful—more capable, and therefore more ready to meet what is before them, than any nation of the world, is due above all else to that faith in man which was the glory of our fathers, and enabled them to found a Government of the people, by the people, and for the people. For to these men the Nation meant the aggregate of the individuals who compose it—each one of those individuals they believed a being capable of indefinite perfectibility; and the Government was neither the Nation nor the Nation's Master, but the Servant appointed by the people, to keep order and prevent the encroachment upon the rights of the individual.

A Government which found its highest honor in serving the people and leaving the individual free to develope his own personality according to the possibility of his capacity, was the ideal of the founders of this Government.

That the times have greatly changed no one can fail to see. The whole tendency of the day is to appeal to the Government to do that which our Fathers never dreamed of as being in its province. That this tendency is likely to increase in the Coming Century, I can not doubt—the whole drift of political thought in Europe and America is toward some form of Socialism. Institutions of Charity which would once have been the gift of individuals are now expected from the town. Local laws which the public opinion of the community will not enforce, the Legislators are petitioned to enact. States are not ashamed to ask aid of the General Government, and industries which would die a natural death because planted in localities where nature is against them, look to the Government to tax the people in order that they may violate the natural law of existence. The fashion having once been set, has been followed in unexpected ways. The workman is demanding that our once hospitable doors be closed against all who will compete with him. In other words, they ask that a Government which was established to cast the shield of its protection over all who sought a home where they might be assured of liberty, and a fair chance to show what was in them, and enjoy the reward of their labors, shall limit that protection to those who have been fortunate enough to rush in before the doors were closed. This is not the place, nor am I the person to discuss the economic bearings of such questions. I only ask to be allowed to call your attention to the fact that the Coming Century has grave dangers—dangers which do far more than affect our economic relations with one another and with the nations of the world. These dangers affect the National Character. We are in danger of substituting for Republican independence, with its buoyant hopefulness, its youthful expectation and its noble faith, a mendicancy which is at once the root and the fruit of a Paternal Government. Our unexampled material prosperity has placed before us an ideal which may be as fatal as Midas' touch. The life of the nation may perish of hunger in the midst of the plenty which will not feed it.

But a far more important question is, what can be done? I answer, that the need of this day and country is an Aristocracy. Not of birth—we have seen what that has led to in France. Not of wealth—we are destined to see that dissolve in England. But an Aristocracy of Character. Whose ranks will ever be replenished by the best blood in the Nation, and whose voice will be lifted up with power to guide the destinies of the people. The first essential of such an Aristocracy is unselfishness. We need men who expect nothing from the government and need nothing. Men who in every village in this land will raise the tone of the community and recall to the people the fundamental object of Government. Let them be physicians or farmers, jurists or teachers, merchants or writers—it matters not—only let them be men of high ideals and fearless courage. Their first work will be to create a new and purer atmosphere. To show to a people feverish for wealth and ready to fall a prey to the charlatan, the power and glory of a life of plain living and high thinking.

There is where the work of the new Aristocracy would begin; but it would not end there. I know that the cry "the gentleman in politics" and "the scholar in politics" is apt to provoke a smile. It is said, "we have seen such but they produced little effect. The politician must not be above his trade. He must creep through the Saloon and shut his eyes to corruption and reward the boys when he wins. The gentlemen and the scholars had better stay at home." That there is truth in such saying we all know. But why is the path to political power low? It is because the desired end is low. If the object of Government be to subsidize monopolies, and pension the slothful, and reward the corrupt, of course only mean and low men can succeed in the low means which are essential for success. But if the object and end of Government be something very different, if the making of the conditions of freedom in a highly complex and widely extended society be the end of Government then there is need of the scholar and the gentleman. Surely they can not expect to succeed simply because they are learned or gentle. They must have the vocation, they must be in the highest sense "available," but for such men there is to-day in this land an opportunity the like of which has never been seen before. We may for a moment turn to our books in disgust, or devote our energies to the accumulation of wealth, but the saying of Aristotle remains true "Man is by nature a political being." To say that men actuated by generous motives and filled with the wisdom which comes from the study of the Humanities have no place in the political life of this country, because for a moment the rewards seem to be for the corrupt, is as wild as to declare that there is no place in war for the genius of Von Moltke or the heroism of Lee, because amongst cannibals he is the successful warrior who can dash out the most brains and most greedily drink the blood of the slain.

Just a Hundred years ago has been called the critical Period of American History. What period is not critical? That crisis had hardly passed when the Nation had to decide whether the plow which had just begun to turn the rich furrow of peace should be laid aside to rescue the sailor from England's tyranny. Scarcely had the young nation begun to grow before the hissings of nullification were heard in the land. And last of all came the appeal to arms. We have never been without a crisis. But what has brought us through? It has been the clear vision of some seer who has revealed to the people the meaning of their destiny, and roused them to the defence of their heritage. The stainless character of Washington was more to the nation than the alliance of France. The profound insight of Jefferson into the meaning of human government; the indomitable will of Jackson which saved the infant Hercules till he might be fit to undertake his heroic labors; the keen American common sense of Lincoln, which like a gleaming axe, split to flinders the sophistries which would have fenced in the nation—whose magnanimous heart would have bound up the wounds of the people, which the rapacious camp followers had torn open that they might rob the wounded and the dying; such individuals have been our salvation and our glory. We have had many crises, but in every one there has come a man equal to the occasion. To-day we need not one but many. "We wrestle not against flesh and blood but against spiritual wickedness in high places."

When we were boys we loved to discuss, is the pen mightier than the sword? To-day in the great Agora of life the question to be decided is, is the corrupt use of money, is the employment of the Government for selfish purposes, is the appeal to the passions of European ignorance, mightier than the virtue, the patriotism and the intelligence of those whose fathers laid the broad foundations of this Government and whose brothers died to defend it?

I can not doubt what the issue will be. Let but one champion arise filled with knowledge, strong in the awful reverence of God, inspired with faith in man, and call on the people to realize their calling, and the waters of patriotism will rush forth as when Moses struck the rock in the wilderness. The people want to do right. They do wrong when some devil has persuaded them that the doing of right is hopeless. The need of the day is a Prophet, a man to speak for God, and when he comes the people will answer him, and the cloudy pillar will lift, and the host take one step more toward the promised land of individual perfectibility.

II. If the need of the day is of a wise and unselfish man to influence our political life, and show again that he that would be great must serve, no less is there need of one with profound insight and infinite patience to disentangle the snarl of our industrial and social life. The youthful hopefulness of the beginning of the Century is in strange contrast to the unrest and discontent which envelope us to-day. The tenement house with its swarming, filthy, shameless population is a blot upon every city in the land. The fearful contrast between the luxury of the rich and the squalor of the poor, the frantic efforts of the laborer to better his condition, the strikes which paralyze the commercial life of the city, the huge combinations of Capital which prevent competition, and are a constant menace to the integrity of Legislators if not to the purity of the judiciary—these are some of the sombre facts which confront us and make us pause in our centennial congratulations, and ask ourselves whether the hopefulness of our fathers was more than the childish anticipation of good which arises from ignorance of evil.

I believe not. I believe the men of a hundred years ago were profound philosophers and far seeing patriots; but the conditions of life have changed to an extent which it was imposible for human foresight to anticipate. The inroad of ignorance is a serious menace to a Republic based on intelligence. The changed character of our urban population offers great temptations to the unscrupulous politician. The selfish display of luxury by a bastard Aristocracy inflames the passions of the unprincipled. The helplessness of the individual in conflict with the trusts, form the standing argument of the Socialist; and the pitiful condition of the poor makes the cry of the communist for any change, which even for a moment will alleviate human suffering find an echo in every manly heart.

The great question of the day is this: Are these evils the natural result of the form of society which our fathers loved? Is the liberty upon which they called unequal to the task of Government, and is the equality in which they believed a dream which vanishes with the realities of practical day? Or, have the conditions so changed and the evils grown so intolerable that we can no longer wait for the slow amelioration of the condition of the poor, but must apply some remedy which is in direct opposition to the theories of society which the wisest men have held? To answer those questions we must find the causes for the inequalities which exist. They are not difficult to find, if only a man is willing to be declared heartless because he insists upon facts.

I believe I know something about the condition of the poor in this country, and I say without fear of contradiction, that as a rule, *degrading poverty*, unless as the result of intemperance, is unknown amongst Americans. As a rule the American workman can take care of himself and his family. In other words, and it is of the utmost importance to bear this fact in mind, the conditions of our American civilization are not such as to crush into poverty the industrious, the virtuous, and the intelligent. These are the men who form the great body of plain people, the very back bone of the community. We still have a great mass of men and women in a dreadful condition, but there is no question that a very large part of this poverty is the result of intemperance and kindred vices. But the residuum is large enough to be appalling, and what is worse it is daily increasing. But these people are not the outcome of Republican civilization, the children of our public Schools, whose fathers spoke in the Town Meeting and whose mothers exercised their souls on the great problems of time and Eternity. The children of The Old Town Folks are not in degradation, nor are the descendants of Cooper's backwoodsmen crushed by circumstance. No, nor as a rule, the offspring of Uncle Remus. They are the proletariat of Europe, a class unknown to our Fathers. They have swarmed from the sewers of Paris, and crawled from the alleys of Naples; they have fled from the bogs of Ireland and burst from Russian prisons; they escaped from the iron imperialism of Germany. They are ignorant, untrained, in spiritual darkness, filled with the hatred of Government as such, for they have never heard of a Government which did not exist to crush the poor; they find themselves suddenly placed in the midst of a highly intelligent, industrious, law-abiding, virtuous people, and they are unable to cope with them in the race of life. Is it strange that it should be so? Would it not be utterly confounding were it otherwise? Let us think of them with infinite pity for they have been brought out of lands of bondage of which we know nothing. Let us strive to help them, filled with an unconquerable hope that each of them has within him the possibility of the Divine Personality. But, when we are told that our boasted freedom and our pretended equality have produced the beggar and the thief, the anarchist and the agitator, we answer no. It is England's misgovernment of Ireland, it is the partition of Poland, it is the ignorance of Italy, it is the vice of Paris, it is the tyranny of Germany, it is the bloodhound cruelty of Russia, that has changed the image of God into this sorry sight.

No, gentlemen, let us beware of panics. There is no need to break up the ship because we find that we have taken on passengers with fever. There is only need that each passenger should do his part in the unexpected exigency. If the history of this country teaches us any thing it is that the pathway from degrading poverty lies through intelligence, industry and virtue to-day as always. Once awake in man the consciousness of his dormant personality in an atmosphere of Freedom, and he will solve the problem of life.

But, we hear it answered, and not by the enraged Agitator, but by serious, earnest, pitiful, intelligent men

longing for the dawning of a better day. " We have no
freedom. The conditions of life are altogether favorable
to the rich and hostile to the poor. No progress is possible until Government assumes the charge of all industries and distributes the fruits equally amongst all the
people." The Political economist may well ask, when
such a scheme is proposed, where is the Aladdin's lamp
which will so greatly increase the effectiveness of industry as to produce such plenty? But I waive that point
and turn to the moral bearing of Socialism. If we find
that the probity of the politician is strained in the attempt
to distribute honestly the country Post Offices, where are
we to find men who could be entrusted with such power
as the Socialistic schemes propose? Taking human nature as it is, Socialism would open a door to rascality such
as the world has never seen. The jobbery under Napo-
leon III. would be economical compared with it, and the
taxes of George III. right in principle and light in weight.
If we wish for the rule of a Rehoboam, let us give up all
things into the hands of a Paternal Government, and it
will say to us "My little finger shall be thicker than my
father's loins. And whereas my father did lade you with
a yoke, I will add to your yoke: My father hath chastised
you with whips, but I will chastise you with scorpions."

All such schemes, no matter how generous may be the
motives which actuate their promoters, are doomed to
failure, for they are essentially unnatural and unchristian.
Unnatural, because nature always has paid and always
will pay large wages to the intelligent, the farseeing and
the industrious. Unchristian, because they are attempts
to produce a moral change by material rather than by
spiritual means.

The difficulties of the day are not few, but let us beware lest we cast away that which has brought us all our blessings. Whatsoever is lovely and honest and of good report in our American civilization to-day is the fruit of a splendid Individualism. Before that, as represented by the New England farmer, and the Virginia rifleman, the compact and well organized civilization of France was swept from this Continent. Before it again the armies of England fell. It was that which made Pickett's charge possible; and it was that too which defended Cemetery Hill. A plain man who little dreamed that he was a hero expressed that which has been our glory: " I stood, he said, by the wall of the peach orchard at Gettysburg, and saw Pickett's men sweep across the plain. I said no army can withstand them, but when they drew near, I said: 'My God, the Union depends upon *me*, and then I could have lifted twenty ton ! ' "

Any re-arrangement of the elements of society which has some other aim in view than the ennobling of character will end as did the French Revolution; and any attempt to improve the condition of mankind which does not set before itself, as the first step, an appeal to what is essentially noble in Humanity is doomed to failure. From that step it would inevitably follow that there would be a re-arrangement of society to express more perfectly the better ideal, and to make the conditions of life more favorable for its continuance.

Now, if we are not mistaken in our reading of the history of the world, and above all, of the history of the last three hundred years, we may be sure that the nobility of which we have spoken must be filled with faith in and love of Democracy. What we need is not less Democracy but more Democracy. Democracy has pushed its way into the Court room and insisted that not only must Justice's eyes be blinded, but that no one must whisper to her whether he who stands at the bar be noble or peasant. Equal justice has been won and the law is respected. Democracy knocked at the door of Parliament and demanded that they who obeyed the laws and furnished the means of existence to the Government should be heard in the making of the laws. So we have political equality and with it peace. Soon Democracy will speak to the new industrial Aristocracy and insist that in some way, those that bear the burden and heat of the day shall have a share in the industrial life different from that which has yet been granted to the workingmen. But the new step onward of Democracy must be taken by itself. It can not be lifted into the promised land by any act of Government, it must pass through the wilderness, but in time it will arrive. What it needs to day is a leader. That is the work for the new Aristocracy.

What we need is better men; above all a new nobility, filled with the spirit of Chivalry, with lives devoted not to the recovery of the Holy Sepulchre, but to the discovery of the manger of Bethlehem in every human heart. When that comes the Holy Grail will be found, and when men drink of it as brethren,—intemperance will flee away, and the exactions of power be ashamed, and the shameless luxury of our bastard Aristocracy will slink away as did the noisy crew when the sweet lady of Milton's Comus walked in their midst without fear!

III. Such a conception of individual value and the strong hope of the improvement of society through the purifying influence of an awakened Personality is impossible apart from faith in the Divine Purpose, belief in the infinite perfectibility of man, and consciousness of the indwelling of the Spirit of Truth. In other words Religion is the first essential for Democracy. For, Democracy is like a brave swimmer, who has cast off all human life-preservers, and committed himself to the waves; firm in the faith in the buoyancy of the waves, the vigor of his own arm and the reality of the land which he hopes to reach.

But the ecclesiastical life has its dangers no less than the political and the social. There is danger lest a panic take possession of men's souls, and faith be divorced from knowledge; lest the test of any advance in knowledge be not its truth but its safety. It is the spirit of fear which leads men to turn to the Scribes, who stand at the temple door, turning over the pages of the past, and ask them whether the new truth glowing with the light of a better day can safely be admitted to the dim religious light of the past. They may keep it out, but with it they will keep out the youth and glory of the Nation. There is great danger lest our Sectarianism dissipate the energy which can be found only in unity. There is danger lest, that being strongly felt, men turn in despair to a great and splendid foreign organization which promises truth but at the cost of liberty.

What is the remedy? It is here as elsewhere, I believe, in a glorified individualism. The world will never hear the Truth proclaimed with authority till it comes like the voice of many waters, till it break upon us like the sound of harpers harping on their harps. The harper touches a single string and if he be a master then the note is true. It is not the Truth, yet *true*. The *truth* is heard when every string has given forth its true note; then in the great symphony the spirit of humanity will cast its crowns before the Eternal throne. All that is in the future. We are not to disregard the past nor the voice of the past—to do so is to produce discord. The past has struck the key note, and we must listen to it. The important thing for every man is not to have the truth but to be true, and out of these individual utterances will come the perfect and satisfying harmony of Humanity. And this thought lifts Truth out of the mystic atmosphere of the schools and brings it into the clear light of life. Every experience that comes to man is the touch of the Divine hand, and every answer to such experience is doing more for the world than all the treatises on philosophy which the world has ever seen.

The same law holds in the life of religious organizations. From the beginning there have been two religions in Christendom, the one a religion *about* Jesus and the other the religion *of* Jesus—the same religion which He had. It is the former which persecutes; the later which conquers. It is the former which has made all the Sects warring one with another; it is the latter which has been the joy and light of man. The religions about Jesus can never have any unity. Each sect says, let us have union by all others becoming such as I am. The unity of the other exists to-day and can never be broken. It is the great company of faithful people found in every sect and every nation. That that Unity should be made more effective no one gainsays. How is it to be accomplished? By recognizing that the members of Christ's Body are not organizations of men for the perpetuation of a dogma, or the preservation of an order, but *individuals* filled with the Spirit of God. Paul said to the Corinthians: Ye collectively are the Temple of the Holy Ghost and members *in particular*. But we have higher authority than Paul. When Jesus had been rejected by the Jewish Church and forsaken by the Galilean multitude, He turned to his disciples and said, "Whom do men say that I am?" What is the popular opinion about me? It made no matter what it was. What say ye. Peter said, "Thou art the Christ." And Jesus said on THEE I found my Church. The Church is founded on individual recognition of the Divine Man and stands or falls according as that foundation is built upon. The unity of the man consists not in the juxtaposition of his clothing whether the hat be a mitre, or the cloak a surplice, or the shoes the pilgrim's sandals. It consists in the living co-operation of the members of his body. Now the sects are to Christ what the clothes are to the man. They can never unite. The members of Christ whether under mitre, surplice or in sandals, are the individual souls for which he died.

Let us not be afraid because we are told that all our woes are the result of individualism: only substitute, for that much abused word, Personality, and we have the key to the questions of the day in Politics, Society and Religion.

Will the Coming Century advance or retrograde? No man can tell; it all depends upon this one question: will the individual more and more realize and make effective his dormant Personality. The schemes of dreamers we need not consider; the advice of Paul is as good to-day as when first given, "Take heed unto *thyself* and to the doctrine."

And where my friends are we to look for men to purify politics, ennoble society and revivify the church? You anticipate me in the answer. It is in the great company of scholars who fill the halls of our colleges and universities.

The relation which a college should hold to the State can not be discussed at the end of an address already too long. But this we may say, that if the object of the State be not merely protection but the return to each individual of that nobler personality which the State embodies, there can be no means so efficacious for that work as education.

Now in a Democracy, the State will be the embodiment of the common ideal. So the State provides for the perpetuation of that ideal in the common schools. But if that be the only means of learning, the education of the children of the Commonwealth will be meagre indeed—it will never rise to the level of that nobler ideal which has been revealed to a chosen few. This fact has been appreciated, and at one time it was thought that Sectarian Colleges would meet the need of the hour, but more and more it is being felt that the Sects as such, are capable of but limited progress, and so we come here as elsewhere to see that the salvation of the college itself must be in the individual.

Let those who have been blessed by our ancient mother join hands to enable her to carry out the ideal which she revealed to us, untrammeled by politics and unbiased by Sect affiliations, and this State will have cause to bless us who have been blessed by it.   The gifts of one man have made Baltimore the seat of an unique and splendid University, where men may investigate to the farthest limits of the human reason every subject which is of importance to the race.   Such an establishment however has not lessened but increased the value of a college in which the minds of boys may be inspired with a love of learning, and trained to discern facts.   Starting on the broad base of the common school system, and passing through the college curriculum to the University, Maryland has opened to her children such a pathway as perhaps can not be found elsewhere in this land.   It will be a fatal thing if for want of means—and that means for want of interest— while the foundation remains and the capital rich with sculpture is ready to be lifted into place, it is found that the aspiring shaft which should unite the two is wanting to the temple of learning in this Commonwealth.

We are assembled to commemorate the founding of an institution of learning older than our Constitution, not to ask that some new work should be begun.   We have heard the roll call of worthy sons who have been born of this ancient mother.   There is one more to be added to them.   Let us not forget, lest we suppose that our Alma Mater is stricken with age, that it was from these halls, aye from the class of '73 that he went forth who bore the Nation's flag through the darkness and horror of the Arctic night, and planted it in the dawn of a new day farthest North. James Booth Lockwood has done more for his day and generation than any of us will ever be permitted to do. For he has shown to a people prone to worship material comfort, and to a generation given to the applause of success, that patient endurance and heroic courage, and self sacrifice, are the things that make life worth living. *Quod homo fecit homo faciat,* was the motto of the class to which he belonged. He fulfilled it. Let us who remain, see to it that other children have the same opportunities to develope a noble character.*

Yet, while we congratulate ourselves upon beign the children of this honored mother, we can not ignore the fact that other colleges have been enabled, through the munificence of individuals, to leave our Alma Mater far behind in the progress of learning. This ought not to be. It was in Maryland that the first step was taken toward laying the foundations of this liberal government.†
May it be her part to lead in the no less noble work of the Coming Century, by the true education of the Personality of her sons.

Too long, O Alma Mater, hast thou lain at the Beautiful Gate of the Temple. Now, in the Name of Jesus Christ—in the Name of that Divine Personality, which was conscious that it was the Son of God and in that consciousness realized its freedom and its power—rise up and

---

* The remains of Lieutenant Lockwood now repose in the Naval Cemetery overlooking the Severn, and almost within the shadow of his Alma Mater. [EDITOR.]

† The meeting of Commissioners to consider the interest of the different States, met, on the invitation of the Maryland members of the Continental Congress, in Annapolis, on Sept. 11th, 1786. This meeting was the first of several which preceded the Convention which framed the Constitution. See The Critical Period of American History, by John Fiske, Boston, Houghton, Mifflin & Co. 1888, p. 216.

walk! In the inspiration of a nobler ideal enter through the Beautiful Gate of Learning into the Temple of God, and stop not till thou reach the Holy of Holies, and bring forth the gifts of knowledge, which will free from super-stition and low living; the lust for gold and the thirst for selfishness, and enrich with love and hope and an un-shaken faith.

At the close of the Oration, the Apostolic Benediction was pronounced by the Rev. CLELAND K. NELSON, D. D., a former Principal of St. John's.

The audience then proceeded across the Campus, Dr. FELL, with Mrs. JACKSON, the wife of the Governor of Maryland, leading the way, to the Tree which had been selected to commemorate the Centenary of St. John's. Standing by the side of Mrs. JACKSON, on a temporary platform, Mr. J. SHAAFF STOCKETT, of the Class of '44, as President of the Alumni Association, spoke as follows:

We are about to crown the very interesting exercises in which we have to-day been engaged, by selecting and setting apart this *tree as a MEMORIAL, to recall to the sons of St. John's, for ages to come, this our first Cen-tennial celebration. And if it prove worthy of its vener-able parent—the Old Poplar—that has weathered the storms of centuries, and around which cluster so many agreeable associations, and beneath whose wide spread-ing branches, many of us, here present, have gamboled

---

* The Memorial Tree was raised from seed obtained by Mrs. Nicholas Brewer from the "Old Poplar."

in our youth, it will afford a grateful shade in the summer's noontide, and perchance, a trysting place in the evening hour, for generations yet unborn.

A grander and more enduring monument, however, than this Memorial Tree, may be wrought out in the future, if, starting with to-day, under the ennobling inspiration of our centennial commemoration, we, the sons and friends of St. John's, resolve to labor in our respective positions, and to the full measure of our ability, to make this, now venerable Institution of learning, a true fountain of knowledge, from whence shall issue a rich stream, widening and deepening as it flows, fertilizing the arid wastes of ignorance, and yielding an abundant harvest of noble men, who by their high culture, their varied attainments, by a true and lofty manhood, shall exercise a large and controlling influence for good, everywhere. I may not, however, enlarge upon this theme, here and now. I hasten to the close.

Mrs. JACKSON, the wife of the Governor of Maryland, has kindly consented to participate in this ceremony of setting apart our Memorial Tree. A lady, who has commended herself to so many of the citizens of Annapolis, as well as to others, by the grace and courtesy with which she has oft dispensed the liberal hospitality of the Executive Mansion, needs no formal introduction from me. She is no stranger to St. John's Boys. Nor are they wanting in appreciation of her friendly interest in their behalf. The Collegian—a member of the graduating class of this year—who, in the athletic sports of a year ago, bore off the prize her hand bestowed, would, I am quite sure, give her his hearty support for any office, to which, in the new order of things—sometimes foreshadowed—she might aspire. And in such event I make bold to say, we all, "with like acclaim" would shout the Jackson name.

At the close of these remarks, PRINCIPAL FELL presented to Mrs. JACKSON a trowel filled with earth, and decorated with the College Colors—Orange and Black. Mrs. JACKSON sprinkled the earth around the tree, at the same time giving expression to the hope that it might long continue a memorial of the day.

At the conclusion of this ceremony, a choral was sung, and amid the hearty cheers of the students, and the College yell, the large assemblage dispersed.

Business Meeting of the Alumni.

In the afternoon, the Alumni Association held a business meeting beneath the marquee. The meeting was called to order by the President. The proceedings of the last meeting were read by the Secretary, James M. Munroe, and, after being corrected, were adopted.

On motion of Frederick W. Brune, the preparation of a Memorial Volume of the Centennial Proceedings, was entrusted to the Executive Committee; and on motion of Henry D. Harlan, a Committee of two was appointed to proceed immediately to procure subscriptions from the Alumni present to meet the expense of publishing such volume. Henry D. Harlan and Frederick W. Brune were appointed the Committee, and they proceeded forthwith to the discharge of the duty assigned them. They presently reported that the sum of $312 had been subscribed, and that an additional sum of $100 had been guaranteed to supply any contingent deficiency.

After other proceedings, the following persons were elected Officers of the Association for the ensuing year:

President.

J. SHAAFF STOCKETT.

Vice-Presidents.

NICHOLAS WALTER DIXON,
JOHN SLUYTER WIRT.

Secretary.

JAMES M. MUNROE.

Treasurer.

LOUIS DORSEY GASSAWAY.

Executive Committee.

HENRY DAVID HARLAN,
LOUIS DORSEY GASSAWAY,
JAMES HARWOOD IGLEHART,
HUGH NELSON,
DANIEL R. RANDALL.

Historiographer.

SAMUEL GARNER.

The Association then adjourned.

The Alumni Banquet.

In the evening in McDowell Hall, at tables arranged somewhat in the shape of a horseshoe, and tastefully decorated with flowers, nearly a hundred persons were gathered to take part in the good cheer provided by the ALUMNI ASSOCIATION of ST. JOHN'S. Representatives of classes extending over half a century, were assembled in loyal friendship to recall the memories of 'the past, and to pledge anew their devotion to their Alma Mater.

Mr. J. SHAAFF STOCKETT, President of the Alumni Association, presided at the festal board, with Dr. Nelson on his right, and Dr. Leavitt on his left. The following persons were present as guests of the Association:

Rev. Cleland K. Nelson, D. D.
Rev. John McDowell Leavitt, D. D.
Thomas Fell, LL. D., Principal of St. John's College.
Captain William T. Sampson, Superintendent of the
    United States Naval Academy.

And the Class that was to graduate on the morrow, namely:

Lemuel S. Blades,
Thomas L. Brewer,
Charles G. Edwards,
Charles H. Grace,
Nicholas H. Green,
Albert H. Hopkins,
William G. T. Neale,
Herbert Noble,
Edwin D. Pusey,
Charles H. Schoff,
John Gibson Tilton,
William E. Trenchard.

At the close of the BANQUET, Mr. STOCKETT arose, and after tendering a cordial welcome to his Brother Alumni, as also to those not of the same Academic household present as guests of the Association, and who by their presence added to the enjoyment of the feast, announced the following toasts:

St. John's College—An institution of learning, that may with a mother's pride, point to those whom she has nurtured, and sent forth well equipped for the battle of life, and say "these are my jewels." This was responded to by Mr. Nicholas Brewer.

The Principal of St. John's—A gentlemen who by his scholarship, and wise administrative capacity, aided by the hearty co-operation of his colleagues, has advanced St. John's to a degree of popularity and usefulness that gives assured promise of a bright future. This was responded to by Dr. Fell.

A Former Principal of St. John's—Who on re-visiting the scenes of his labors and work, has brought as a .

tribute to the centennial festival, a Poem abounding in thought, stirring in sentiment, and clothed in language chaste and felicitous. Dr. Leavitt responded to this toast.

The Faculty of St. John's—A band of competent and faithful instructors, who discharge the duties of their respective positions with high credit to themselves, with great benefit to the students, and to the honor of the College. This was responded to by Professor Charles W. Reid, M. A., Ph. D.

Our Alma Mater—Weakened by many conflicts in the past, and sorely tried by neglect, she now stands forth encouraged and stimulated by her work already accomplished, resolute to achieve greater and more brilliant results in the future. Response was made to this toast by Dr. Abram Claude, Mayor of Annapolis, of the Class of '35.

The Old Poplar Tree—"The groves were God's first temples," and this stately pillar of great Nature's Church, remains the only witness of the birth and growth of our time-honored Institution. Responded to by the Rev. Vaughan S. Collins.

Our New Members—May you "leave behind you footprints on the sands of time." Mr. Nicholas H. Green of the Graduating Class, responded to this toast.

Mr. Frederick Emory—An alumnus whose chaste and polished address before the Philokalian Society, of which he is a member, aptly illustrated the influence of the Love of the Beautiful. This was acknowledged by Mr. Emory.

Rev. Leighton Parks—Whose eloquent and philosophic address to-day, commanded the admiration of his auditors, and enlarged the reputation of his Alma Mater. Responded to by Mr. Parks.

Mr. Philip R. Voorhees—An alumnus, to whom St. John's cheerfully acknowledges her indebtedness for his accurate, comprehensive and valuable historical sketch of the College, delivered at its Centennial Celebration. This toast was responded to by Mr. Voorhees.

Professor Samuel Garner of the United States Naval Academy—A graduate of St. John's devoted to the profession of teaching, the foundation for which was laid at his Alma Mater. Responded to by Professor Garner.

During the evening the following was sung:

Song

For the Reunion of the Alumni.

———

Air :—Maryland, My Maryland.

———

To thee we come from far and near,
   Alma Mater, bearing
Each his gifts, to lay them here,
   Each thine honors sharing.
At thy feet once more we sit,
   Find, each year returning,
The torch at which our lamps we lit
   Still serenely burning.

Afar we see thy beacon light,
  Hear abroad thy praises;
Oh, feed that holy flame aright,
  Till none more brightly blazes.
We, enkindling here anew
  Light of thy bestowing,
Bear us as thy servants true
  On thine errands going.

Fill us with the highest things,
  O benignant mother,
All that lifts man, all that brings
  Brother near to brother.
Spread the truth that maketh free,
  Night to daylight turning ;
Let the world receive from thee
  Noblest fruits of learning.

Now, in thy memory-haunted hall,
  Alma Mater, meeting
On thy Centennial, one and all,
  We offer thee our greeting.
Oh, may thy life for ages run,
  And show the path where virtue leads,
A beacon-light, a glorious sun,
  A fruitful source of noble deeds !

Another day had entered on its course before the Festal Board was deserted, and the Alumni of St. John's separated, carrying with them a lively remembrance of the commemoration of the FIRST CENTENARY of their Alma Mater.

𝔑𝔞𝔪𝔢𝔰

OF

GRADUATES AND OTHERS, PRESENT AT THE ALUMNI BANQUET.

Arms, Francis Thornton
Basil, Jr., Joseph S. M.
Blades, Lemuel S.
Boswell, H. Heber
Bowie, Robert
Brewer, Charles, M. D.
Brewer, Nicholas, M. A.
Brewer, Jr., Nicholas, B. A.
Brewer, Thomas Leverett
Brooks, Nathan C., M. A.
Brown, Robert Riddell, M. A., LL. B.
Brune, Frederick W., B. A.
Brune, Thomas Barton, M. A., M. D.
Chapman, Marshall, B. A.
Claude, Abram, M. A., M. D.
Claude of A., Dennis
Claude, Gordon H.
Collins, Vaughan S., M. A.
Crabbe, Walter R., B. A.
Daley, Charles F.
Dawkins, W. J., M. A.
Dixon, Nicholas Walter, B. A.
Dubois, Charles A.

Edwards, Charles G.
Emory, Frederick
Fell, Thomas, LL. D.
Frick, George A., B. A.
Garner, Samuel, B. A., Ph. D.
Gassaway, Louis Dorsey
Gassaway, Louis G., B. A.
Grace, Charles H.
Greene, James B.
Green, Nicholas Harwood
Green, Jr., Richard H.
Green, Thomas Kent
Griffith, H. L.
Hammond, Edward
Harlan, Henry David, M. A.
Harlan, William H., B. A.
Harlan, W. Beatty, M. A.
Harter, George A., B. A.
Hicks, Thomas H., B. A.
Hopkins, Albert Hersey
Hutton, Orlando, D. D.
Iglehart, James Davidson, B. A., M. D.
Iglehart, James Harwood, LL. B.
Leavitt, John McDowell, D. D.
Magruder, Jr., John R.
Marchand, George E.
Mullan, John, M. A.
Munroe, Frank A.
Munroe, James M., B. A., LL. B.
Murray, James D.

Murray, Jr., James D., B. A., LL. B.
Neale, William G. T.
Nelson, Cleland K., D. D.
Nelson, Hugh, M. A.
Noble, Herbert
Parks, Leighton, M. A.
Pusey, Edwin D.
Quynn, H. H.
Randall, Blanchard, B. A.
Randall, Burton A., M. A., M. D.
Randall, Daniel R., B. A., Ph. D.
Randall, John Wirt
Randall, Wyatt W., B. A.
Ray, John G., B. A.
Reid, Charles W., M. A., Ph. D.
Ridout, John, B. A.
Ridout, William G., M. A., M. D.
Roberts, G. C.
Sampson, Captain William T., Superin-
    tendent U. S. Naval Academy.
Sasscer, Frederick, M. A.
Schoff, Charles H.
Slade, H. M
Stockett, Frank. H., M. A.
Stockett, Jr., Frank. H.
Stockett, John Shaaff, M. A.
Stockett, Thomas R., M. A.
Thompson, James Guy
Tilton, John Gibson
Trenchard, William E.

Tuck, Philemon H., M. A.
Voorhees, Philip R., M. A.
Wathen, F. Eugene, B. A.
Wilmer, Joseph R., B. A.
Wilson, J. S.
Wirt, John Sluyter, B. A.

Commencement Day.

THURSDAY, 27TH JUNE, 1889.

After the usual exercises the following Degrees were conferred:

Graduating Class.

Bachelor of Arts.

CHARLES H. GRACE, Bozman, Md.
NICHOLAS HARWOOD GREEN, Annapolis, Md.
ALBERT HERSEY HOPKINS, Baltimore, Md.
HERBERT NOBLE, Port Deposit, Md.
EDWIN D. PUSEY, Princess Anne, Md.
WILLIAM E. TRENCHARD, Church Hill, Md.

Bachelor of Science.

LEMUEL S. BLADES, Bishopville, Md.
THOMAS LEVERETT BREWER, Annapolis, Md.
CHARLES G. EDWARDS, Baltimore, Md.
JOHN GIBSON TILTON, Norfolk, Va.

Bachelor of Letters.

WILLIAM G. T. NEALE, Upper Marlboro', Md.
CHARLES H. SCHOFF, York, Pa.
JOHN GIBSON TILTON, Norfolk, Va.

Other Degrees were conferred as follows :

Mechanical Engineer.

JOHN H. BAKER, Assistant Engineer, U. S. Navy,
Washington, D. C.

Master of Arts.

JAMES DAVIDSON IGLEHART, Class '72, Baltimore, Md.
JOHN SLUYTER WIRT, Class '72, Elkton, Md.
NICHOLAS WALTER DIXON, Class '77, Crisfield, Md.
LOUIS DORSEY GASSAWAY, Class '81, Annapolis, Md.
GRAFTON J. MUNROE, Class '82, Springfield, Ill.
CHARLES BREWER, Class '85, Annapolis, Md.
JACOB GRAPE, Jr., Class '86, Baltimore, Md.
WILL BUSH SHOBER, Class '86, Cumberland, Md.
CLINTON T. WYATT, Class '86, Goldsborough, Md.

Honorary Degrees.

Master of Arts.

ROBERT BROOKE DASHIELL, Ensign, U. S. Navy,
Annapolis, Md.

Doctor of Divinity.

REV. RANDOLPH W. LOWRIE, Bennings, D. C.
*REV. WILLIAM SCOTT SOUTHGATE, Annapolis, Md.

Doctor of Science.

REV. WILLIAM C. WINSLOW, D. D., S. T. D., Ph. D.,
L. H. D., LL. D., D. C. L., Boston, Mass.

Doctor of Laws.

REV. JOHN McDOWELL LEAVITT, D. D., Brooklyn, N. Y.

Doctor of Philosophy.

THOMAS FELL, LL. D., Principal of St. John's College,
Annapolis, Md.

---

*The like Degree was conferred on Mr. Southgate on the same day, by his Alma
Mater, Bowdoin College.